FATE'S
Rendezvous

B. K. JONAS

ISBN-10:978-0692475225
ISBN-13:0692475222

DEDICATION

Fates's Rendezvous is dedicated to the romantics in the world. May you continue to romance and be romanced.

CONTENTS

ACKNOWLEDGMENTS

Writing a book is truly a collaborative effort requiring praise and thanksgiving. I begin mine by thanking God for planting the seed of desire and the creativity required to complete the task. I encountered many paths before coming back to my first love of writing before giving myself permission to pursue this journey.

I thank my husband, Alonzo, daughters, Antoinette and Arica, my mother-in-law, Helen, and my sister, Barbara for believing in me and supporting me as I wrote and shared snippets along the way. Your confidence and feedback inspired me to "finish the book."

Kathy, thank you for giving me my first book on freelance writing eons ago. That book opened the door for many more and fed the seeds already planted. Thanks, too, for putting me in touch with Sharon L. Clemens.

Sharon L. Clemens, I appreciate that you shared your story and answered all my questions.

I send special thanks to Officer Lester who answered all my police protocol questions and guided me in getting the details right in *Fate's Rendezvous*. I have many more questions for an upcoming novel.

Terri, you were a Godsend to me, reading and critiquing chapters along the way. You inspired me each time you asked for more.

Myra, thank you for introducing me to Trice Hickman and for reading and critiquing as I wrote.

Trice Hickman, thanks for your wisdom, kind words, and encouragement along the route.

Jerrica, thanks for the Frozen Imagery photography and artwork. You made the cover design and us look great!

And finally, I thank other friends, family members, previous students and social media friends who waited patiently for me to "finish the book" so they could purchase their copies, and I could begin my next novel.

May you enjoy reading Bianca and Jeremiah's story as much as I enjoyed writing it.

B. K. Jonas

CHAPTER ONE

Bianca smiled to herself as the wheels of the plane touched down on the runway at Houston Intercontinental Airport. She was almost 1000 miles away from her real home, but Houston had been a second home for her ever since she'd first traveled home for spring break with Marissa, her college roommate sophomore year. Well, except for that one summer, when she'd avoided Houston altogether--but she didn't want to think about that now. Home was where you came to nurse your wounds, recover from stressful situations, and just to be loved unconditionally. And right now, Bianca needed all three of the above. Although nearly, a year had passed, she'd yet to recover from the lies that had led to her break up with David. When their relationship had ended, she'd been collecting data for her doctoral dissertation which then needed to be analyzed in order for her to actually write the results and consequently graduate. Because of the level of attention required at that time, Bianca hadn't had the time or energy to mourn the loss of her relationship with the man with whom she'd expected to spend the rest of her life. He had proposed to her hadn't he? Had she been wrong to expect to be the only woman in his life?

Even David's friends had told her they thought he was crazy for cheating on her. His best friend had told her, "Bianca, David is crazy. Most men would kill to have a woman like you. You're fine, intelligent, and determined to accomplish your dreams. What he did is about him and not about you. We've been friends since junior high, but what he did is wrong, and there is no other way to call it. You need to get over him and his doggish ways, and just keep it moving."

Now that Bianca had earned her doctorate degree and procured a contract with a quickly approaching deadline from a publishing company, she needed to complete her manuscript on the case studies

1

of the teachers she'd interviewed. During her sabbatical from her position as assistant professor of education at Benson College, she would now get the chance to visit with her longtime friend, relieve the stress of the past few months, and write her book. She could not have planned a better vacation.

Eager to greet Marissa, yet dreading the line to exit the plane, Bianca waited patiently for those already standing to pass her seat before she stood to retrieve her overnight bag from the overhead storage compartment. Armed with the overnight bag and her carry-on bag which held her laptop and purse, she made her way down the narrow aisle of the plane.

*****

After entering the airport, Bianca followed the mass toward the baggage claim area. Knowing Marissa, Bianca expected she'd run into her before she actually reached the baggage area. Whenever she visited, Bianca would tell Marissa to just meet her outside in the passenger arrival area to save parking costs, but Marissa always met her in the passenger arrival area just past the security gates, so Bianca expected Marissa to do the same this time.

Bianca was surprised to find that she made it all the way to the baggage claim area without meeting up with Marissa. Perhaps Marissa had heeded her advice and was indeed waiting in the car. That would be a first. As she stood waiting for her bag to be added to those circling the carousel, her vision was suddenly blocked.

"Marissa, I know it's you, Girl." Bianca laughed while reaching up to grab the hands that blocked her view and turning simultaneously to hug her friend.

"Hey, Girl! How was your trip?" Marissa asked the question without waiting for an answer and continued speaking. "I was late leaving the house so I couldn't meet your flight. I almost called you to cancel your trip, but I thought, 'What the heck? You deserve a break anyway!' Steve had to leave yesterday to go to Paris to take care of some business for his job, and since they'll pay for me to join him, I'm catching a flight later tonight…"

"Hold on. Hold on. Hold on. Slow down, Marissa. What are you talking about?"

"Let's get your bags in the car and grab a cup of coffee. I'll tell you all about it.

*****

A half hour later, Bianca was still numb from the news Marissa had given her. "So you really think it's okay for me to stay at your place while you're gone? I guess it wouldn't be the first time. But I was really looking forward to spending time with you and Steve."

"Look, Girl. You'll be fine. And you must admit you really do need this trip. If I'd written a 250 page research paper, I'd have taken a trip as soon as it was approved. Not to mention that mess caused by that David whatever his last name was. Did I tell you I never did like him? Look, Mom knows you're coming. And so does Mrs. Roberts. I left their numbers and directions to their houses near the phone in the kitchen 'cause I know you never remember how to get to their houses. You can sleep in the den or in our room. Make yourself at home. Steve has a phone we can use for international calls, so I'll call every few days. And I'll let you know when we're coming home as soon as I know the date. Steve said it could take two weeks or more to clear up the mess. But, Girl, you know I couldn't pass up a free trip to Paris, France. Paris, Tennessee I could miss.

*****

Two hours and two cups of coffee later, Bianca watched as if in a daze when Marissa went through the security gate toward the plane that would take her to Toronto for her connecting flight to Paris. Emitting what her colleagues deemed as one of her signature sighs, Bianca headed for Marissa's car. In one hand she held her purse and the directions to her vacation home. In the other, she held the keys.

Bianca had no trouble following Marissa's directions, especially since she'd made the trip on numerous occasions though she'd only driven the route a few times by herself. Once she exited the freeway, the route became completely familiar. The popular drive-through hamburger restaurant and the Certified Store marked her right turn leading toward the subdivision of homes where Marissa and Steve had built the one they'd designed. Silently, she recalled which homes belonged to which neighbors. She didn't remember everybody's names, but she could recall most of them. It had only been a year since her last visit, but that one had been a short one due to the death of Marissa's father. It had been five years since Bianca had visited just for the fun of it.

The motion activated flood lights mounted on the house and garage came on as Bianca entered the driveway from the street allowing her to view the exterior changes her friends had made since her last visit. She knew Steve had done the landscaping because whenever she and Marissa talked, Marissa complained about the exorbitant price of one plant or another. Bianca had never ceased to be amazed by the flowers that bloomed in Houston even during the winter months. Now, bright peach Day Lilies lined both sides of the semi-circular drive. Pink rose bushes outlined the wall of the family room which connected the garage to the rest of the home. Palm trees dotted the massive yard. Way too much yard for a city girl like Bianca, but she had to admit it was beautiful. In fact, the layout of the trees, tropical plants and flowers created a haven which even a city girl like her could appreciate.

Bianca opened the garage door with the remote she found above the visor and pulled the Mercedes inside. Grabbing her bags, she proceeded to enter the house. Once inside, she continued her mental inventory of the changes. Marissa had always been fascinated by antiques, and her home reflected a comfortable mix of contemporary and antique furnishings. Bianca would not have thought the two styles complimentary until she'd seen Marissa pull it off.

Bianca noted that hardwood floors had replaced the carpet from earlier years in the open family room. One wall of the family room held an elaborate walnut entertainment center which housed a 51-inch flat screen television, DVD player recorder, Blu ray player, and a Bose stereo system. Bianca admired the technology and looked forward to watching movies in peace. Her friends and family members often teased her about never sitting still long enough to watch a movie simply for the sake of enjoyment. Usually, she was reading, writing, or grading papers while she watched television or movies. That's why it often took her three or four attempts to actually view a movie in its entirety.

Once she'd unpacked the few items from her overnight bag and hung her clothes from the garment bag, Bianca called first her parents back home in their respective Chicago suburbs, and then her sisters in Washington, DC, and Italy to tell them she had made the trip safely. The way everyone made her check in reminded Bianca that no matter how old she got, she would always be the baby of the family. When she finished calling her family, she would've called Marissa's mom to say hello and to let her know that she was settled in, but she remembered the late hour and decided to call the next morning.

As she prepared the sofa bed, she wondered why Marissa had given her the choice of sleeping in the den or Marissa and Steve's bedroom. When Bianca had visited on previous occasions, she'd always slept in the guest suite which consisted of a bedroom, sitting area, and a private bath. After making sure all the lights were out in the house and the doors were locked, Bianca returned to the den with intentions of going directly to sleep. When she turned off the light in the ceiling fan, the blinking red light on the answering machine caught her attention. She knew she'd never be able to sleep with that light illuminating the room, but she didn't feel comfortable checking Marissa and Steve's messages. She could probably just write any messages down, but it would just feel like getting into her friends' business. And, anyway, Steve or Marissa might be waiting for particular messages and be planning to check their messages from Paris. The thought occurred to her that she could just cover the machine to block out the light like she covered the light emanating from her laptop when she went to bed at home. Technology was wonderful, but the nightlights drove her crazy.

In bed again, she tried to fall asleep, but the papers she'd placed over the light only seemed to diffuse the light more, making it appear as a large blinking blob on the ceiling and wall. After tossing and turning for over an hour, Bianca covered her face with her pillow. Only then was she able to fall asleep.

*****

Jeremiah exited the freeway and headed toward his cousin's house. He could hardly wait to hit the shower and remove the grit from his body. He'd been driving for twelve hours straight, two hours over the family company limit, and he could honestly say he understood why guidelines for truckers were set. His family owned the company, and they'd set the guidelines, but Jeremiah had to admit he'd pushed the envelope tonight. Trucking was hard work, but he appreciated the freedom it gave him from the nine-to-five routine of working in the office. Jeremiah could almost thank Samantha Gold Diggin' Travis for inadvertently pushing him to return to driving three months ago.

He could hardly believe he and Samantha had made plans to spend the rest of their lives together. He was glad he'd discovered her true colors and her true agenda before they'd made it to the altar. Henceforth, he would steer clear of highly educated "citified dames". Give him a good old-fashioned country girl any day. Someone who held good old-fashioned morals and values. Someone like his cousin's wife, Marissa. Jeremiah thought he'd met someone like that for himself years ago, but she'd proven him wrong. But Jeremiah tried not to think about that part of his life.

Jeremiah parked his truck in the area he'd come to know as his spot since temporarily moving in with Steve and Marissa and headed toward the house. In a way, he was glad Steve and Marissa were out of the country because he was not in the mood to talk to anyone tonight. For some reason, today had been unusually harrowing. He was really looking forward to the next two weeks off. He needed to check on the status of his home and to take care of a few business matters. But right now, he just wanted to clean up, eat, and sleep.

*****

Bianca woke with a start after it seemed she'd only just fallen asleep. The last thing she remembered was trying unsuccessfully to block out the blinking light from Marissa's answering machine so she could get some much needed sleep. She recalled how she hadn't been able to get any relief until she'd covered her face with a pillow.

Immediately alert, she lay still trying to quiet the resounding beat of her heart as she attempted to identify what had roused her from her slumber. Over the sound of her heartbeat, she heard a noise from the other side of the door to the den. It sounded like someone was in the family room. Rising up slightly, she stared toward the closed door as if doing so would allow her to hear more clearly. There it was again. It sounded like someone placing things on a table. Who was out there? Bianca was supposed to be in the house by herself. Both Marissa and Steve were away for who knew how long. If she could just get out there to see who it was. But what if she startled the person? Whoever it was could have a gun or a knife, and she could be killed. But she couldn't just hide out here in the den while her friends were being robbed blind.

Slowly, Bianca got out of bed and crept to the phone. For the first time that night, she was glad for the blinking red light that guided her. As quietly as she possibly could, she grabbed the cordless receiver and tiptoed to the double closet doors. After opening one of the doors and stooping beneath the clothes, she dialed 911 leaving the closet door slightly ajar so she would hear if the prowler ventured toward the den.

"Nine-One-One Emergency. How may I help you?" The dispatcher responded after one ring.

"I'm visiting at my friends' house, and there's a prowler or a burglar in the house." Bianca whispered feeling she couldn't give all the details without alerting the prowler. "Please come quickly. I'm alone." She really just wanted to ask for help and hang up, but apparently that was not the preferred procedure. The dispatcher calmly instructed her to stay on the phone until the officers arrived so that they could be sure that she remained safe.

Bianca answered the dispatcher's questions as quietly as she could. She understood that the dispatcher's responsibility was to calm her down while she kept her on the phone, but Bianca had no intention of letting whoever was in the family room know that she was in the den or that she was alone. When the dispatcher repeated a question, Bianca almost snapped at her from the tension she held at bay. It was not easy to listen to the person on the phone with one ear and her unwelcome intruder with the other ear. She could hear movement but couldn't actually make out what the person was doing. It sounded like he was cooking. But what kind of prowler cooked himself a meal before stealing the goods? Bianca was truly baffled.

After hearing a few seconds of no sounds, Bianca thought that perhaps her prowler had left, but then she heard what sounded like voices from the television. This was the weirdest burglar she had ever heard of. First he cooked? Then he watched television?

Over the muffled voices coming from the television, Bianca heard the doorbell ring. In a few seconds, it rang again. It was obvious that her visitor was not answering the door. A few seconds later, Bianca heard what sounded like someone banging on the front door. Following that, she heard louder voices.

The dispatcher on the phone informed Bianca that the officers were in the house. She asked again where Bianca was located in the house. After a few seconds during which it seemed that the dispatcher was speaking to someone else, the dispatcher informed Bianca that it was safe for her to go into the family room.

Grabbing her robe from the closet hook and throwing it on, she walked slowly out of the den into the adjoining family room. She was not sure what she expected to see, but it certainly wasn't what she saw.

Standing in the middle of the room stood a half naked man with his hands in the air. On the top, he wore nothing but bulging muscles. On the bottom, yellow smiley faces in a background of red peeked out over thread bare blue jeans clearly thrown on in a hurry. Under any other circumstances, Bianca would have ogled a man dressed in that manner, but the current situation kept her from enjoying the view. The muscle definition in his back, his rear end, and in his thighs, made it look like he was posing for one of those magazines over which her friends in college had drooled. Okay, her, too.

Facing the prowler were two police officers with guns raised but not actually pointing at the prowler. One officer stood a couple feet from the man. The other maintained a position closer to the door.

"What's going on here?" The prowler asked.

"We got a call about a prowler, and we had to check it out."

"So who called the police?" The officer closest to the front door asked.

"I did." Bianca offered, inching her way into the family room.

"Who are you?" asked both officers and the prowler simultaneously.

"My name is Bianca Jefferson. " The nearly naked man was gorgeous from the front, too. A low haircut tapered into sexy sideburns which framed a caramel complexion accented with a slight moustache and neatly trimmed beard. Hazel brown almond shaped eyes glared beneath long thick lashes women would kill for. "I....I'm visiting from Chicago." As she spoke, Bianca watched as the prowler's eyes first got wide and then formed slits. As they did, recognition dawned. The prowler was not a stranger after all.

"Bianca Jefferson! Talk about a blast from the past! You've got a lot of damn nerve showing up here after that disappearing act you pulled ten years ago!" He snapped at Bianca.

"Jeremiah? Jeremiah Davis? What are you doing here?"

"What do you mean, 'What am I doing here?' This is my cousin's house. What are you doing here?"

"Ma'am, Mr. Davis here has already verified who he is and that he is currently living here. He has identification and receives mail at this address. What about you?"

"I have identification, but I'm just visiting with my friends, Mr. Davis's cousins."

"How are you visiting Steve and Marissa when they're out of the country?" Bianca had never heard Jeremiah so angry. She realized she did not like his tone aimed at her.

"Can I put my hands down?" He asked the officers. It was obvious to Bianca that Jeremiah wanted to make no mistakes.

"Marissa met me at the airport and gave me her keys after explaining that she was going to join Steve in France." With the prowler who had become Jeremiah looking at her, Bianca began to wish she had put her clothes on instead of just grabbing her robe. She felt as undressed as he looked. "I saw her off before coming here. I can prove it. I put her keys right there on the counter in the kitchen." She nodded indicating the breakfast bar on the other side of the room. "My ID is in my purse in the den." She answered.

"Ma'am, if you would get the keys and your ID, we can check them out. Sir, you can put your hands down."

Bianca walked to the kitchen to retrieve the keys and handed them to the officer. Before turning to retrieve her purse and ID, Bianca looked toward Jeremiah. She hadn't meant to look directly into his eyes, but she did. Under different circumstances she could drown in those hazel eyes. In fact, she'd done just that on more than one occasion. But that was definitely a lifetime ago. The anger she saw there now made her heart beat even more rapidly than it had before she'd initially recognized her prowler.

"Check these out," the officer said to his partner, handing him the keys from Bianca.

The partner checked to see if the keys fit the door locks before nodding to the officer nearest Jeremiah and Bianca.

"Well, there certainly seems to be some kind of mix up here," the officer stated as he handed Bianca her ID and keys. You both seem to be who you say you are. Mr. Davis is clearly living here. Ms. Jefferson, it seems you are the one for whom we have to take your word that you belong here. Do either of you have a phone number where we can contact the homeowners?"

"I have Marissa's cell number in my phone. I don't know it by heart. And I have another number Marissa gave me to reach them, too," Bianca offered.

"I have Steve's number, too."

"If you two could get those numbers, we'll try and contact the homeowners to verify that you both should be here."

Bianca went back to the den and copied Marissa's cell phone number and the new number Marissa had given her on a Post-it note and returned to the family room. She saw that Jeremiah had also written a number on a Post-it note. As they both handed the officer their Post-it notes, Bianca's hand brushed Jeremiah's, and she could've sworn she felt an electrical shock, but neither of the men acted as if anything out of the ordinary had happened.

The officer handed the Post-it notes to his partner saying, "Call these numbers and see if you can get in touch with the homeowners. If not, just leave a message. Ask them to call the station as early as possible. Call in her ID, too."

The partner stepped back outside to make the calls. A few minutes later he came back inside and called the other officer over to his side.

After they exchanged a few brief words, the leading officer addressed Bianca and Jeremiah. "Well, my partner was unable to reach the homeowners. He did get their voice mails so he left messages at all of the numbers. Based on the fact that you both have keys, that Mr. Davis is living here, and that you have no warrants out for your arrest, there is nothing else we can really do until we hear from the homeowners. Perhaps, you two can just work this whole thing out. If not, one of you needs to get a hotel room until your friends return. You can always call us back if there are any problems." With that, he turned to leave, closing the door behind him.

Bianca stood watching the door, stunned. How in the world was she supposed to stay in the house with Jeremiah Alfonso Davis after what had happened ten years ago. When had he moved to Houston? And specifically to Marissa and Steve's? And why hadn't Marissa said anything about him? At least Bianca now knew why Marissa had told her to choose between the den and the master bedroom. She couldn't believe she had almost had Steve's cousin arrested. She turned to face Jeremiah, trying to think of a way to apologize for the mishap, but all she saw was the closing of the door to the guest suite.

Jeremiah closed the door leading into the guest suite making a point of not slamming it. He didn't want his unwanted roommate to know just how much she'd ticked him off. He didn't want to give her the power of knowing she could affect him the way she did after all these years. He was over one Ms. Bianca Denise Jefferson. He had gotten her out of his system almost ten years ago.

Like it was yesterday, he could still remember driving to Steve's apartment to pick Bianca up for their date only to find that she'd left town and returned home. Afterward, he'd felt like a fool with the dozen roses on the front seat of his mustang and the velvet lined box in his pocket. When Marissa had handed him that plain white Number 9 envelope from Bianca, his heart had imploded. He'd read that damn letter so many times he'd memorized it.

*****

Dear Jeremiah,

This is probably the hardest letter I have ever written or will ever write. These past couple of months have been like a dream come true for me. Who would have ever thought when I came down here for my internship that I would meet someone as special as you? You are the type of young man that every young woman dreams about. On top of being intelligent and handsome, you are kind, considerate, compassionate, patient, and above all a Christian. I expect that you have other positive traits that I have not witnessed first hand.

I know that you think you are in love with me, but I feel that we have not known each other long enough for you to be in love with me. I have strong feelings for you, also, but I think that is because of the amount of time we have spent together this summer. I am sure that once I go back to Chicago and you start graduate school, you will forget all about me.

If I were finished with my undergraduate degree, we could probably go to graduate school together, but since I have two more years to go, I do not feel it would be fair to ask you to wait for me.

By the time you receive this letter, I will have already left Houston. I would appreciate it if you would let me go and just forget about me. You will always hold a special place in my heart.

Bianca

*****

Jeremiah still kept that letter and the ring in his safety deposit box at the bank to remind him of what happened when you gave your heart away unconditionally. How dare Bianca show up here just when he was getting his life together again! And how dare she try to have him arrested in his own cousin's house! Women! What made them think that they were always in the right, and men were always against them? He definitely would call Steve in the morning to make sense of this. He definitely didn't want to spend the next two weeks with an unwanted house guest by the name of Bianca Denise Jefferson. And why'd she look better now than she had when he'd last seen her? The way Jeremiah felt now, he was almost willing to call a competitor to get a job that would get him back on the road again. He could just postpone his much needed vacation until after Ms., no Dr. Jefferson left. How dare she show up here after ten years!

*****

Bianca started to knock on the door of the guest suite, but quite honestly, she was afraid of the response she'd get. How in the world had she ended up here with Jeremiah after purposely avoiding him for years? She had been so excited about her upcoming book publication and her much needed sabbatical that she hadn't even thought to inquire about Jeremiah as she'd done before visiting in the past. Suddenly, she was too tired to think. All she wanted to do was get some sleep. She'd tell Jeremiah how sorry she was in the morning. Perhaps, she'd even make breakfast for him. She was sure Marissa had a well-stocked refrigerator.

Returning to the den, Bianca glanced at the blinking red light and decided she was not going to fight with it anymore. Pulling a pad from the desk drawer and a pen from the cup on top of the desk, she poised herself to write down the messages.

"Bianca! Bianca! It's Marissa. I forgot to tell you. Jeremiah's been staying with us for the past few months. You know how we are. Always got a house guest. Anyway, Jeremiah's driving a truck, and he's away a lot, but he should be back soon. So don't have a heart attack if you come home one day and find him in the house. We gave him the guest suite. Talk to you later."

Laughing, Bianca deleted the message and climbed into bed. If Marissa had told her about Jeremiah while they were still at the airport, Bianca knew she probably would've paid the extensive exchange fees to return home immediately. But she was a big girl. She could handle being there with Jeremiah until Marissa and Steve returned. At least that's what she told herself. In any case, she owed

Jeremiah an apology. Two actually, but he'd get one tomorrow. If she got her way, they would never discuss the first apology she owed him. As she drifted off to sleep, Bianca wondered why in the world would Jeremiah, a Harvard MBA graduate, be driving a truck.

~~~~~

CHAPTER TWO

Jeremiah woke to the smell of bacon and French Vanilla coffee. At first he thought he was dreaming, but then he remembered everything. The police. And Dr. Bianca Denise Jefferson. Like a blast from the past. Bianca from Chicago. All the way here in Houston, Texas to haunt him as she'd done for years. Jeremiah thought he'd gotten over being in love with Bianca, but his reaction to seeing her last night told him he'd only been fooling himself. With her smooth bronze complexion and those slanted chocolate brown eyes set above high cheekbones, Bianca was still one of the sexiest women Jeremiah had ever met. Even in satin pajamas, a velvet robe and a "do rag," Bianca looked more beautiful than many of the women he knew who spent hours in front of a mirror trying to look good. Jeremiah had been captivated by Bianca's looks when she was still a teenager. The woman he had faced in the wee hours of the morning took attraction to a whole different level.

What Jeremiah couldn't understand was how he could've even noticed what Bianca looked like under the circumstances. The woman had almost had him arrested. And in his own cousin's house. He should've had her arrested years ago for what she'd done to his heart. In all honesty, he suspected that the police would've had him committed to a mental institution if he'd tried to have her arrested back then. What would the charge have been? She'd absconded with his heart? Jeremiah shook his head as he thought about the fact that he currently had all of his liquid assets tied up in the building of his new home. If it weren't for that, he would seek refuge in a hotel just as the police officer had suggested.

He convinced himself that since he'd only be here two weeks before he was on the road again, he could manage to be in the house with Bianca. He needed to find out how long she was going to be here. Maybe she'd be gone when he came back from his next trip.

She couldn't have more than a couple week's vacation. Surely, she'd just come from Chicago for a quick visit as she'd done periodically over the years. Oh, he'd not seen Bianca for years, but Jeremiah had heard bits and pieces about her from Steve and Marissa over the years. He knew she'd earned her bachelor's degree in education and had gone on for first her master's degree and then her doctorate. She'd taught public school for a while before going back to teach at her alma mater where she'd met Marissa. He hadn't heard anything about her getting, married, so Jeremiah assumed she was still single. But then again, since he'd never asked Steve or Marissa about Bianca directly, she could've gotten married and he just didn't know. He and Bianca just needed to stay out of each other's way, and they could live in his cousin's house temporarily. He just needed to get his brain and body working together so he could stop his brain from venturing down that path of "what if's." The past was exactly that, the past.

After showering, dressing and making his bed, Jeremiah allowed his hunger pains to lead him toward the smells of breakfast that had wakened him. He couldn't hide in his suite forever. It didn't help that the grumbles in his stomach wouldn't be ignored no matter how unhappy he was with his unwanted roommate. They were adults. Surely, they could work out a temporary housing situation.

As soon as Jeremiah left his suite, he spotted Bianca in the kitchen. Now she was dressed in tight jeans and a red sleeveless top that highlighted the curves the robe had only hinted at last night. Her hair was still tied with the blue and white bandana. He smiled to himself as he noted it really wasn't a "do rag."

Bianca lifted her head and stopped the beating of something in a bowl that Jeremiah assumed were eggs. Behind her, he could see a griddle on the stove.

"Good morning, Jeremiah," Bianca spoke hesitantly, not knowing how Jeremiah would respond. She quickly washed and rinsed her hands in the sink and dried them on a hand towel. "I'm really sorry about that whole mess last night, or early this morning. I can't tell you how sorry I am. I really didn't know you would be here at Marissa and Steve's. Allow me to make it up to you with this peace offering of breakfast." She indicated the table already set for two.

Determined to fight the physical attraction he felt toward Bianca, Jeremiah slowly crossed the floor of the open family room and entered the dining room. "Is there something I can do to help?" He asked thinking that helping Bianca was the last thing on his mind.

"No. I'm just about to make western omelets. You do eat those don't you? I've made pancakes, bacon, and coffee. You can fix yourself a cup. I'm on my second cup already." Bianca returned her attention to the bowl of beaten eggs after turning on the stove. Even though he'd asked to help, it was obvious to Bianca that Jeremiah wasn't comfortable talking to her. And he hadn't actually accepted her apology. Surely, he wouldn't hold last night's fiasco against her forever. More than likely, Bianca realized, to Jeremiah, last night's fiasco was just icing on the cake considering the manner in which they'd parted ways.

When the eggs were ready, Bianca joined Jeremiah at the table where he sat drinking his coffee. She noticed he'd poured pineapple-orange juice for both of them. She brought the pancakes from the oven and warmed the maple syrup in the microwave. By tacit agreement they began fixing their respective plates. It occurred to Bianca that this might have been a snapshot of their life had she not run scared all those years ago.

Expecting that Jeremiah might just be too angry to pray with her, Bianca silently blessed the table and then began eating. She hadn't thought about it when she had set the table, but with Jeremiah directly across from her, he was in her natural line of vision when she looked up from her plate. And what a vision it was. Though he was fully dressed, Bianca recalled how he had looked in nothing but boxers. Muscles rippling across his broad shoulders. And then his physique when he had turned...that washboard stomach. Bianca worked out every day and had yet to achieve that effect. Why was it that men seemed to get better as they aged while women just aged?

Just then Jeremiah raised his head, and their gazes locked. Bianca could feel the heat rising to her cheeks. It was a good thing for her Jeremiah couldn't read her mind. She did not want him to know that she'd been mentally undressing him. She smiled nervously averting her eyes.

"So, Jeremiah, what brings you to Steve and Marissa's at this time?" Bianca asked trying to begin a conversation. Maybe if she could get him to talk to her, they could start to get along again.

"I'm between homes." Jeremiah responded tersely. No reason to tell her everything. He wasn't going to be around long enough to tell her his whole life story. Besides, he'd done that already, and where had it gotten him?

"You know me. I'm just visiting again. I'm on sabbatical from my job. How long will you be here?" It was obvious that Jeremiah was not in the mood to talk to her. The Jeremiah, she knew was quite loquacious and was often the life of the party. Bianca hated knowing that she was probably the reason for his change in demeanor.

"Not sure."

*****

After several unsuccessful attempts at engaging Jeremiah in meaningful conversation, Bianca gave up and finished her meal in silence. She had no intention of begging him to talk to her she didn't care how fine he was or how inviting his cologne made him smell. She just thought that since they'd be living together for the next few weeks, they could at least be civil to one another in spite of their past. She couldn't help it if she'd been raised to be cordial, and he hadn't. She was not sure how long she could stay in the house with Jeremiah if he refused to talk to her, but she would not make a decision to leave just yet. She would settle in and perhaps by the time Marissa and Steve returned, things would be better. She did not have time or energy to deal with the likes of Jeremiah Alfonso Davis. She'd apologized for almost getting him arrested hadn't she? It had been a natural human response to call the police on him, hadn't it? How was she supposed to know that Jeremiah would be in town visiting Marissa and Steve when she arrived? She had successfully avoided crossing his path for ten years, timing her visits to Houston specifically when she knew he was in Dallas, Cambridge, or better still, out of the country on some sort of international business. Why now had fate turned against her? Last she'd heard, he was some big wig in his family's trucking business in Dallas.

"Thanks for breakfast," Jeremiah said to her as he rinsed his dishes and put them in the dishwasher.

Bianca had been so engrossed in her internal monologue that she hadn't realized Jeremiah had finished eating.

"You're welcome," she responded looking up as Jeremiah loaded the dishwasher. I'm impressed, she thought to herself. A man who knows where to put dirty dishes. It might not be much, but it was more than David knew. He had expected her to cook and wash the dishes afterward. Jeremiah had even offered to help with breakfast. That was definitely a point in his favor if anyone were counting points, which she certainly was not doing.

Jeremiah closed the door to the guest suite praying that distancing himself from Bianca would help him to forget the heat that had passed between them when their gazes had locked across the table. He was in no mood to allow himself to be sucked into the dream that was Bianca again, but apparently his body had a mind of its own. From her deep brown eyes, high cheek bones in caramel colored skin to her slim waist, tight buns and everything else in between....In any case, he had a full agenda for the day. He had no time to drool over his unwanted roommate...almost ex-fianceé. He and Bianca had talked about a future together, but she'd never given him the opportunity to formally propose. No she'd just left that damn letter for him. What a fool he'd been. He definitely did not have time for that! He had too much business to tend to. His first stop was to check on the progress of his home. During the past week, the builder's site engineer had left several voice mail messages for him regarding matters on which he needed Jeremiah's input.

*****

After loading her own dishes into the dishwasher and cleaning the table and stove, Bianca poured herself another cup of coffee and went to the den to unpack her remaining clothes and office equipment for her short visit. Most of the clothes from her rolling Pullman she hung in the den closet. It looked like Marissa had removed clothes from half the closet just for her because clothes hung on only one side of the closet. Bianca had no doubts that prior to her planned visit, Marissa's extensive wardrobe had filled the entire den closet as it undoubtedly filled the other closets in the house. Steve frequently joked that he and Marissa had a five-closet household in which he was allowed to use one fourth of the master bedroom closet. Bianca had teased him once telling him that she knew of a couple husbands who had to use closets in other rooms so he should consider himself lucky that he got to use part of the master bedroom closet. Steven had not found that funny.

Bianca's toiletries easily fit on and in the guest bathroom vanity. However, she had to move a few things to make room for her laptop and portable printer on the desk in the den. Bianca knew that

Marissa and Steve had a computer and a printer in their home office, but she preferred to use her own equipment than to rely on that of others. It was just easier for her to depend on her own equipment when she traveled. She knew from experience that computers and printers all operated with their own idiosyncrasies, and the last thing she wanted to do was to break her friends' equipment. If her own laptop or printer decided to act up, then she might use Marissa's, but she suspected that she would feel more comfortable looking for a twenty-four hour copy center.

When Bianca finished arranging her temporary living environment, she worked on her manuscript for an hour until the muscles in her shoulders tightened causing her to stop and stretch. She had written a day-by-day schedule of what she needed to complete to meet the deadline she'd set for herself which would allow her manuscript to be completed a month before it was due to her publisher. Saving her material and shutting down her laptop, she decided she'd take a walk and then a hot shower before taking a short drive to reacquaint herself with the community. She'd heard the front door close while she was working, so she expected that Jeremiah had left the house.

*****

After driving around for almost an hour, Bianca decided to end her tour by visiting Marissa's mom. As she headed toward Mrs. Jones's home, she remembered that after the excitement last night and the tension that morning, she'd forgotten to call either Marissa's or Steve's mom that morning. She decided she'd visit Steve's mom later that day or the next depending on how long she spent with Mrs. Jones. But she promised herself that she'd call Mrs. Roberts that day for sure.

Mrs. Jones was working in her garden when Bianca pulled into her driveway. Mrs. Jones waved to Bianca while simultaneously standing and walking toward the end of her garden hose that was lying in the yard. As soon as Bianca was out of the car, she called out to her.

"Why hello, Miss Bianca. Let me wipe the dirt from my hands so I can give you a proper Texas greeting. She rinsed both hands with water from the garden hose and dried them on a towel she pulled from a pocket on the apron she wore as she walked toward Bianca. When she reached her daughter's longtime friend, she pulled her into a bear hug and patted her on the back. When she released her tight hold, she kissed Bianca on the cheek. "My, my, it is good to see you. What a blessing it is that you could come to visit with us. How is your family? Come on in and tell me how everybody is doing?"

As Bianca followed Mrs. Jones into the house, she noted that Mrs. Jones did not look as aged as she had during Bianca's last visit when she'd come for the funeral of the late Reverend Jones almost a year ago. He'd succumbed after a long battle with prostate cancer. Bianca smiled as she took in Mrs. Jones's neatly curled hair and the dress beneath her apron. Mrs. Jones was the only person Bianca knew who perfectly groomed herself to work in the garden. It was no wonder Bianca had never seen Marissa in jeans or sweats.

"Everybody's okay, "Bianca stated as she tried to assist Mrs. Jones with coffee for the two of them. "How've you been?"

"I've been fine. You go sit down. Of course I've had to get used to being here by myself, but I've been keeping myself busy so I don't miss Clarence so much anymore." As she spoke, she prepared two cups of coffee and brought them to the dining room table on a small tray with cream, sugar, teaspoons, and two slices of apple pie warmed in the microwave. "I've forgotten how you like your coffee. I also brought us some pie, too. I made this last night. I've got a few errands to run, but we've got time to enjoy a cup of coffee and visit a while. You're looking good although it seems you've lost a few pounds since I last saw you.

"I was under a lot of stress while I was working on my dissertation, so I lost weight." Bianca had no idea how much Marissa had told her mom about Bianca's experience with David so she was purposely vague. "But I'm picking it back up slowly," she continued. "I'm sure I'll gain a few more while I'm here. I always do," Bianca chuckled indicating the apple pie Mrs. Jones had given her.

"How long will you be here? Marissa said you were taking a sabbatical."

"I am on sabbatical. I'll be here until the Monday before Thanksgiving. My sabbatical officially started a month ago, and I have two more months to go, but I promised my mom I'd help cook Thanksgiving dinner."

"That's great then. You'll be here for Marissa and Steve's annual

Pre-Thanksgiving party.

"I'd forgotten about their party since I've never been able to make it. My mom is a real stickler about family being together for Thanksgiving. Of course, I didn't know Marissa would be gone when I got here. Marissa said she probably won't be gone longer than two weeks. She'd better get back here soon to plan that party."

As Bianca spoke, she thought about Marissa reiterating that she expected to be back within the next couple of weeks when she'd called while Bianca completed her walk that morning. Marissa and Steve had called Officer Johnson back that morning and assured him that Steve and Bianca both had permission to be in their home while they were away. Of course, Marissa found the whole situation with Jeremiah funny. Laughing hilariously, she'd told Bianca, "I would love to have seen Jeremiah in his skivvies with his hands raised in the air." Marissa had apologized for forgetting to forewarn Bianca about Jeremiah living with her and Steve temporarily. Marissa had ended their conversation by saying, "I'm sure you two will get along just fine...You know we never really talked about what happened between the two of you. When I get back home, we are going to 'have that talk'. Something must have happened between you two that you never told me about."

"Marissa has been planning that party for months, so all they have to do is show up." Mrs. Jones added bringing Bianca back to the present before changing the subject. "Well, at least it's good Jeremiah is there so you won't be totally alone. Have you met him yet?"

"Last night," Bianca answered almost choking on her answer as she remembered that Mrs. Jones had not known about her brief romance with Jeremiah the summer she'd visited with Marissa and her family while also completing an internship at Reverend Jones's church. In fact, she and Marissa had purposely kept information about Bianca's relationship with Jeremiah from Reverend and Mrs. Jones because they had not wanted Marissa's parents to form unsavory opinions of her. There was no doubt in the young ladies' minds that Marissa's parents would have considered Bianca a loose woman from Chicago for spending so much time with a man she'd just met. Bianca hated giving Mrs. Jones the impression that she'd just met Jeremiah the night before. But under the circumstances, she couldn't see any other way to deal with the issue. Nor did she feel the need to disclose the details of the circumstances under which they'd met last night.

"It's good you met. I wasn't sure if he was in town now or not," Mrs. Jones continued, seemingly oblivious to Bianca's small white lie. "His schedule keeps him away a lot. I know. Why don't I cook dinner for the two of you tomorrow? I haven't had an opportunity to make anybody a big dinner in a while. How about that?"

Bianca had been having a difficult enough time trying not to think of Jeremiah without Mrs. Jones bringing him up. And, now, Mrs. Jones was inviting the two of them to her house for dinner tomorrow. "That should be fine," she responded amazed that she had not revealed her true feelings which were that she had no desire to be with Jeremiah in the company of her best friend's mom. There was no telling how Jeremiah would treat her.

"Come on, Bianca, let's go. I've got a couple stops to make, and then we can stop at Kroger's to get the rest of the things I need for tomorrow. I'm getting excited just thinking about it. Won't we have fun?"

Bianca did not share Mrs. Jones's enthusiasm, but she certainly couldn't disappoint her so she accompanied Mrs. Jones on her errands. All the while, she pondered how to handle the upcoming dinner with Jeremiah at Mrs. Jones's house.

*****

Jeremiah had just finished his meeting with the site engineer and was climbing into his Jeep Grand Cherokee when his phone rang. He was so set on answering the call before it went to voice mail that he didn't check the caller ID to see who was calling.

"Hey, Man, I just heard you almost got arrested last night." Steve was laughing so hard, Jeremiah could hardly understand him, but he knew his cousin well enough to figure out the gist of what he was saying. Steve had barely given him time to say, "Hello" before guffawing in his ear.

"Hah. Hah. Ha. Man, it was so not funny. Man, why didn't you tell me Bianca was coming to visit? I could've delayed my vacation. As it is now, I'm not sure I can pick up another trip on such short notice."

"Aww, Jeremiah. Don't do that. You know Bianca is good people. I don't know what happened with you two, but right now, she's in the same boat as you. Both of you just broke up with your significant others. Man if you do something to make Bianca leave before we get home, Marissa is going to blame me. I do not want to be in Paris with my wife and have her mad at me, if you get my drift. You two were crazy about one another when you met. The two of you need to make up or something. Trust me when I say, she needs rest and a relaxing environment as much as you."

*****

After talking with Steve for almost half an hour, Jeremiah felt a little better about the situation with Bianca. Apparently, she'd recently broken off a long-term relationship just as he'd done. Steve had shared details about how Bianca had caught her fiancé having dinner at a fancy restaurant with another woman six months before their wedding date. Bianca had found out later that her fiancé and the woman had been involved for almost a year. And to top it off, the guy had been engaged to the other woman, too. Steve wasn't sure how Bianca had ended up at the restaurant in order to catch her fiancé, but she'd undoubtedly been crushed. Steve had shared with Jeremiah that Bianca's trip to Houston was part of her therapy to get over her broken heart.

Before hanging up, Jeremiah had promised Steve that he would not leave the house and that he'd make every effort to get along with Bianca even if only to keep from getting Steve in trouble with Marissa. Jeremiah just hated to admit even to himself that he was still attracted to Bianca after all these years. Not just attracted. He still had feelings for her even after she'd turned her back on their relationship as if it had never existed. It was going to be hard enough living under the same roof with Bianca after their history. But now, after talking to Steve, Jeremiah felt like he wanted to protect her and keep her safe from men who would take advantage of her.

*****

Three hours after leaving Mrs. Jones's house, Bianca was still wrestling with the idea of a cozy dinner at Mrs. Jones's table the next day. She'd visited with Mrs. Roberts and simply passed time after their brief errands, mostly which involved shopping for the next day's dinner. Bianca was so worried that Mrs. Jones would pick up on the mixed vibes emanating from her and Jeremiah that she didn't know what to do. Obviously, she and Jeremiah were drawn to one another physically. They'd always been drawn to one another. But now they could barely hold a civil conversation with one another. What was really difficult for Bianca to understand was why she couldn't just deal with Jeremiah like she dealt with the men on her job or the students she taught. Even as she thought the question, she knew the answer. Mostly it was because she'd never felt confident in relationships with men out of the work arena. But it was also because of the history they shared and the manner in which she'd run away from him avoiding his phone calls until he'd given up and stopped calling altogether.

From their initial meeting when Steve had introduced them at a graduation party held in Jeremiah's honor, Bianca had been attracted to Jeremiah. At first, she'd attributed it to the fact that he was older and more mature than the males she'd encountered in high school and at her college. After all, he'd just graduated from college while she'd only just completed her sophomore year. Later, she'd come to learn that Jeremiah's confidence and self-assurance had allowed him to behave in ways not consistent with the other males in her life. He hadn't had to play games to get people, especially women, to like him. He could just be himself and people flocked to his side, males and females. That personality trait was undoubtedly one of the reasons he'd done so well in international business.

The more she thought about it, the more Bianca came to understand that her reaction to Jeremiah was not one of teacher to colleague or teacher to student. It was clearly a reaction of a young vibrant woman to a gorgeous, sexy man. The truth was Bianca had never responded physically to any man the way she responded to Jeremiah. Not even David had affected Bianca the way Jeremiah did, and she and David had been engaged. The unfamiliarity of that situation was notably the scariest aspect of all. Her sisters would know what to do. Both of them had been fighting men off all of their lives. When the three of them had gotten together when they were younger, Celeste and Serena had been quite open about their attractions to various males, but Bianca had never joined in on their stories. Her sisters had teased her about being too private. Bianca had never corrected them by telling them that she wasn't being private, she'd just had nothing to share. She'd never told them that other than that one summer with Jeremiah, she couldn't relate to their experiences.

What Bianca and Jeremiah had shared had truly been special. They'd been like soul mates. Bianca smiled as she remembered their first kiss. It had been truly magical. One moment they'd been gazing into each other's eyes as they danced to one of her favorite Luther Vandross songs. The next, she'd been wrapped in Jeremiah's arms. Their lips had touched lightly at first, but then what had begun as a chaste touch of their lips had quickly catapulted into an earth shattering, toe tingling event. To this day, Bianca didn't know who'd made the first move. That kiss had marked the beginning of the most amazing time of her life. Her entire summer had been so enchanted it was almost surreal. As the years had gone by, Bianca had convinced herself that her memories had to be products of her over active imagination.

No, Bianca had never revealed any details from that summer with her sisters. When Celeste and Serena had talked about their romances, Bianca had just listened and commented on what they'd shared.

As Bianca saw her current situation, she had two choices regarding how to handle the dinner Mrs. Jones was planning for her and Jeremiah. She could either approach Jeremiah and discuss her concerns---recommending a truce,—or she could let things happen naturally and risk letting Mrs. Jones find out they were not getting along. Or worse yet, let Mrs. Jones witness the simmering attraction between the two of them.

*****

When Bianca arrived back at Marissa's house after stopping for a brief visit with Steve's mom, Jeremiah was watching a movie in the family room. "Good afternoon. How was your day?" she asked attempting cordialness. Bianca chuckled to herself when she realized the movie Jeremiah was watching was one starring Harrison Ford. Men were men everywhere and shared a common attraction to adventure and espionage. Even when they'd dated that summer eons ago, Jeremiah had always grumbled when it had been Bianca's turn to pick the movie they saw. He'd accused her of always picking chick flicks.

"It was fine. How about yours?" Jeremiah responded without taking his eyes off the television screen. Knowing what he now knew about her situation with her ex-fiancé, Jeremiah was afraid that if he looked into Bianca's eyes, he'd see the pain that he'd obviously missed the night before and that morning. He knew if he looked at her now and saw that she was hurting, he might just pull her into his arms to keep her safe. If he did that, he knew he'd wind up being putty in her hands. Again.

"It was fine. I spent part of the day with Mrs. Jones. We ran errands and went to the grocery store. She's cooking dinner for us tomorrow. I wanted to talk her out of it, but she got so excited about the idea, I decided that it wouldn't kill us to enjoy a home cooked meal with a sweet elderly lady. She wants us there at six o'clock."

~~~~~

CHAPTER THREE

Jeremiah turned toward Bianca and watched her retreat to the den. As he watched her, he wondered how he could feel so protective of her even after all these years and what had transpired between them. He realized that if Bianca had tried to talk Mrs. Jones out of cooking dinner for them, Bianca must be as uncomfortable about being in his presence as he was being in hers. Of course, he suspected that Bianca's reasons were different from his. He thought he should probably call Bianca back into the room so they could talk things over. He was just not sure what to say. It wasn't her fault that they'd ended up at Steve and Marissa's together, unchaperoned. Where had that come from? It wasn't as if they were going to jump in the sack with one another. They were adults, and he could surely ignore what seemed to be a natural physical attraction to a sexy woman. The fact that he still had feelings for Bianca was going to be the hardest part to deal with. When he'd turned and faced Bianca the night before, it was almost as if they'd been transported back in time.

He remembered all too well when he'd first laid eyes on Bianca. He'd been at his graduation party given by his aunt and Steve when Steve had walked in the back yard with Marissa and Bianca. Steve had told him he was bringing Marissa's friend from Chicago, but Steve hadn't said anything else about Bianca. Jeremiah recalled how he'd been speaking to a couple of his boys when Steve had entered the yard with the women. When Jeremiah saw Bianca, he lost his train of thought and couldn't even finish his sentence. The guys had teased him at first, but when they'd looked in the direction Jeremiah was looking and saw Bianca, they understood.

After Steve introduced Bianca to everyone, Jeremiah expected her to act stuck up or out of place in the back yard barbecue, but she fit right in, laughing and joking with everyone as if she'd known them for years. Furthermore, he and Bianca had clicked right away, and he'd asked her for a date that same night. All that summer they'd been inseparable. They'd each been completing summer internships, but after work, they'd been together. They'd hung out by themselves. They'd hung out with Steve and Marissa. And they'd hung out with other young people near their ages. They'd just had fun. Jeremiah had learned that Bianca was as beautiful on the inside as she was on the outside. He'd also learned that she was altogether unaware of the sexual appeal she exuded, often stopping men in their tracks when they passed her. And Jeremiah had fallen in love. And he'd thought Bianca had fallen in love with him, too. When she'd left, he'd been devastated.

No, Jeremiah couldn't blame Bianca because he'd not been able to get her out of his head or his heart during the ten years since they'd last seen one another. It wasn't his fault either because God knew he'd tried. He'd even gone so far as to get engaged to another woman to prove he was over Bianca. Not allowing himself to venture down that path, Jeremiah decided that he'd just talk to Bianca in the morning before dealing with the builders again. The fact that he and Bianca had ended up at Steven and Marissa's together, alone, was just one of those tricks of fate that no one could control. How in the world was it possible that Bianca looked even better now than she had before she'd reached the legal age of 21? Who looked that good in a bandana anyway?

*****

The next morning, when Jeremiah came into the kitchen to make coffee, he saw that Bianca had already made a pot. At least it seemed as if she'd made a pot, but about half the coffee was missing, leading him to believe she'd already drunk a few cups. He called out to her, hoping they could talk before his morning appointment with the builders, but apparently Bianca had left the house as he received no response. After peeking into the den, Jeremiah saw that the sofa bed was made up, and the room was empty. He checked the rest of the house, and found that indeed Bianca was gone. Jeremiah decided they could talk later on, perhaps before they went to Mrs. Jones's house for dinner.

As he drove to the site of his new home, Jeremiah thought again about what Steve had told him about Bianca and her ex-fiancé. His friends always accused him of being a softy, but he just hated to hear about women being mistreated. His sisters and female friends always complained about there being a lack of good men available. From where Jeremiah sat, there seemed to be more gold diggin' women on the prowl than decent women who appreciated a man for who he was and not how many letters he had after his name or the number of zeroes he had on his bank statements. But even that did not give men valid reasons to take advantage of women. One thing Jeremiah's dad had taught his sons was that men had to provide for and protect their women. His mom had taught them that their women should help to carry the load. Jeremiah and his siblings had watched their parents work side-by-side to build their trucking business that now had offices in three states. He knew what he wanted out of a marriage was not just a fantasy; he was a product of what he believed in.

From what Steve had told Jeremiah, Bianca had been engaged to her fiancé for almost a year before she'd learned that he was cheating on her and had been doing so for most of their relationship. No one deserved that sort of dishonesty. Jeremiah knew first hand that Bianca was "good people." The fact that she'd remained friends with the Jones family all these years confirmed those beliefs. The Jones family tended to surround themselves with loving people. Once they opened their hearts to someone, that person became part of their extended family. Jeremiah could not remember the names of all of the non-blood family members of the Jones's that he'd met over the years. Bianca was the only one he'd been drawn to from the beginning. Based on the frequency of Bianca's visits over the years, Jeremiah knew that the Joneses viewed Bianca as an extension of their family. It was obvious that they loved her and she loved them back. Bianca was exactly the type of person his friends and family would welcome into their fold.

Jeremiah chuckled to himself as he thought about the fact that none of his family or friends had had two kind words to say about Samantha. Apparently, he was the only one who had not seen her for the money hungry, ladder-climbing person that she was. Jeremiah expected that if he and Samantha had gotten married, she'd be busy spending his hard-earned money decorating their four or five-bedroom home designed by architects for display and not for living. Samantha certainly would not want to ruin her perfect body having any of the two or three children he wanted to have. Bianca's ex had to be a fool for not being able to see the gem he'd had in Bianca.

Smart, beautiful, caring, and sexy.

Jeremiah knew first hand that Bianca's beauty radiated from within and that she didn't spend a lot of time in the mirror adding artificial beauty. He had learned that during that one summer long ago. Unless, Bianca had changed her entire personality over the last ten years, Jeremiah knew that most women could not hold a candle to her. He would've given anything to have been engaged to someone like Bianca. In fact, if Jeremiah had had his way, he and Bianca would've been married almost ten years and probably would have two children by now. The thought of Bianca pregnant with his child made Jeremiah realize the direction his mind was taking. Quickly he reminded himself, that Bianca was like family to the Joneses, and he'd better get his mind off the path it was taking, no matter how sexy she was. If he didn't, it was going to be difficult for him to keep either of his promises to Steve.

*****

Bianca arrived at Mrs. Jones's an hour earlier than the designated time to help with any last minute details. At least that was the excuse she told her longtime friend and surrogate mother. The real reason was she hadn't wanted to deal with the awkward decision of whether or not she and Jeremiah would ride together or take two cars and arrive at the same time. The latter would surely send up a red flag to Mrs. Jones. Bianca did not want the mother of her longtime college friend to know that she and Steve's cousin were barely speaking to one another. Mrs. Jones would not understand why two house guests could not be civil to one another. That just didn't happen in her world.

After informing Jeremiah of the invitation the night before, she'd quickly retreated to the den and had left the house early that morning before he'd gotten out of bed. When Bianca had returned from her morning, run and workout in the park, Jeremiah was gone. In her efforts to avoid Jeremiah, she'd quickly showered and taken her laptop to the neighborhood library to work.

Bianca had finished the salad and was setting the table when she heard a vehicle which she suspected was Jeremiah's Jeep Cherokee pull into the driveway. She purposely allowed Mrs. Jones to answer the door, timing her short walk to the refrigerator for the iced tea with when she expected the doorbell to ring.

"Good evening, Mrs. Jones. These are for you." Bianca heard Jeremiah say before she heard what she recognized as a kissing sound.

"Why, thank you, Jeremiah. You're such a sweetheart. Come on in. We're almost ready to sit down to eat. You can wash up in the powder room."

"You're welcome, Ma'am. I'll do just that."

Bianca could hardly believe this was the same Jeremiah who was sleeping in the guest suite at Marissa's. The same Jeremiah she had dated a lifetime ago. She couldn't see him yet, but the voice sounded the same only without the gruffness to which she'd recently become accustomed. Of course, if she were to be honest with herself, the Jeremiah she had known ten years ago had been a sweet, kind, and romantic individual. Bianca couldn't help but feel a little guilty as she thought about the distinct probability that she was a major contributing factor to Jeremiah's current gruffness. She looked up as the man in question headed down the hall toward the powder room. It was Jeremiah all right. She would recognize that physique anywhere.

"Look here what Jeremiah brought me. Flowers. Why I can't recall the last time a gentleman brought me flowers. Let me put these in water." Mrs. Jones spoke as she pulled a vase from a shelf in the pantry.

As Mrs. Jones worked with the flowers, Bianca continued pouring tea. "I'll get the bread. You go on and have a seat, Mrs. Jones."

"Hi, Bianca. I got your note, so I knew you were here already," Jeremiah addressed her as he entered the dining room as if they were the best of friends. "I hadn't expected that we'd bring two cars." When he had seen the note taped to the door to the guest suite, he swore his heart had skipped a beat in anticipation of experiencing déjà vu.

"I wanted to help Mrs. Jones, so I just left that note." Bianca responded purposely avoiding making eye contact with Jeremiah.

A few minutes later they were all seated at the dining room table and were just beginning to enjoy their meatloaf, mashed potatoes, tossed salad and dinner rolls when Mrs. Jones asked, "Well, Jeremiah. How do you like our Bianca? We just love her. And we have ever since she first came home from college with Marissa. Reverend

Jones and I have always felt like she was another daughter. I'm surprised the two of you never met before. Bianca visited us pretty regularly over the years."

Bianca almost choked on the tea she was sipping. What began as a quick glance at Jeremiah became more when his expression of first complete bafflement and then obvious pain clearly informed her that he'd not known that Reverend and Mrs. Jones had been unaware of their long ago romance. She could feel the blood rush to her cheeks. This was one of those times when she wished for a trap door beneath her seat. How had she missed that Jeremiah had not known that the Joneses were in the dark about their relationship? At that moment, Bianca was pretty sure she did not want to hear what Jeremiah thought of her. In fact, she was pretty sure Mrs. Jones's ears would ring from whatever he had to say.

"Oh, I like her just fine, Ma'am," Jeremiah responded apparently recovering from his shock. "Did Bianca tell you how we met?" He continued. Though his question was aimed at Mrs. Jones, his eyes never left Bianca's.

Silently Bianca pled with Jeremiah to not go there. Didn't he know Mrs. Jones would be horrified and would probably lose respect for Bianca if she knew that she had been involved in a clandestine romance with him so soon after meeting him? Why did he think they'd never met at Marissa's? Or that he'd never taken her home?

"No, I don't believe she told me that story. Why don't you tell it, Jeremiah?"

"Well," Jeremiah started and paused, maintaining Bianca's gaze a moment longer before turning to face Mrs. Jones again. "To make a long story short, Bianca almost had me arrested because she thought I was a burglar."

"Is that right? Bianca didn't tell me that." Mrs. Jones looked at Bianca with a question in her eyes.

Bianca released the breath she hadn't realized she was holding. Obviously, for whatever reason, Jeremiah was going along with the ruse that they had only recently met.

"Well, there I was watching the Chicago Bears game I had recorded, and the next thing I knew, Smokey Joe was busting in the door aiming 357 magnums at me. I didn't even know Bianca was in the house. Apparently, she didn't know I was there either. I guess Marissa forgot to tell her I'd be coming in. And they forgot to tell me about her.

"Well, I'll say. That must have been quite a fright." Mrs. Jones chuckled.

Thank God, Jeremiah had left out all the details regarding the near arrest. No need for Mrs. Jones to know he was nearly naked when they had met. "They didn't really bust in the door," she added to the story. "You actually had to open it. And their guns weren't aimed at you," she added with what she hoped sounded like simple ribbing.

"Bianca, you mean to tell me Marissa never said anything about Jeremiah staying with her and Steve?"

"I think she was so excited about going to France she just forgot. She did call and leave a message on the answering machine though, but I didn't play it until the whole thing was over."

"She did? You didn't tell me that!" Jeremiah eyed Bianca suspiciously.

"Well, if I remember correctly, you weren't speaking to me at the time." Bianca answered returning his glare.

"Well, I can imagine not." Mrs. Jones offered.

"But we made up the next morning, and I forgave her for the whole thing." Jeremiah continued.

Somehow, Jeremiah's version was a lot different from hers, but Bianca was glad they'd cleared that hurdle. She only wished she'd had the foresight to warn Jeremiah that Mrs. Jones didn't know of their previous relationship. She hated being the cause for Jeremiah to lie, even by omission.

Mrs. Jones chuckled to herself as she pushed back her chair promising to bring back the lemon meringue pie she'd baked from scratch.

From the time Mrs. Jones left the room until the time she returned with the pie, Jeremiah stared at Bianca silently pleading with her to say something—anything, that would redeem herself.

"Oh, let me get the coffee, Mrs. Jones." Bianca spoke already pushing her chair back as soon as Mrs. Jones set the pie on the table. She was mortified about the situation and could not handle Jeremiah's accusing look any longer.

How she made it through dessert, Bianca wasn't sure, but when they all had finished, she quickly began clearing the table. "You two go on in the den and visit a while. I'll just take these to the kitchen," she said as she continued with her task. Her hopes were that Jeremiah would actually leave while she was cleaning up from their meal.

Dreading the inevitable confrontation with Jeremiah, Bianca took unusual pleasure in the mundane duties of loading the dishwasher. Rinsing one glass and cup at a time, then the plates-- dinner and dessert--she placed each item in the dishwasher. As long as she lived, she would never forget the look of pain etched on Jeremiah's face the moment he realized Mrs. Jones thought he and Bianca had only just met two days ago. Bianca had been so worried about Mrs. Jones picking up on the negative vibes between her and Jeremiah, she had never thought about the possibility that Jeremiah might not know that Mrs. Jones and the reverend had been purposely kept in the dark about their previous relationship. She could only imagine the thoughts going through Jeremiah's head. More than likely, he thought she'd been ashamed of him. Or worse, yet... that she'd used him and had never really loved him as she'd declared.

Continuing with the silverware, which she placed upside down one at a time in the individual openings of the plastic holder on the bottom rack, Bianca added soap and started the dishwasher. When she'd started the dishes, she could hear Mrs. Jones and Jeremiah talking and laughing in the den although she couldn't make out their conversation. As she began running water in the sink to wash the pots and pans, she realized that she didn't hear any more talking, but she attributed that to the noise level of the dishwasher. At that moment, Mrs. Jones joined her.

"It looks like Jeremiah is having a bit of a problem with his truck. It won't start, so he needs to ride back to Marissa's with you. He said he'll get someone to come here tomorrow and look at his truck since it's almost ten o'clock. Why don't you run on now. I'll finish in here. I told Jeremiah I would send you right out."

That one question—Why don't you run on now--posed as a statement, dashed any hopes Bianca had of delaying her confrontation with Jeremiah. As her mom would have said, it was time for her to pay the piper. As she headed for the door, it occurred to Bianca that she would bet her check that nothing was wrong with Jeremiah's truck.

*****

The tension in the car was so thick Bianca would not have been surprised if Jeremiah's fumes had fogged the windows. After fastening her seat belt, she stared straight ahead as Jeremiah settled in the passenger front seat.

Bianca realized she had felt less tense when she had been worried that Jeremiah was still angry with her for almost getting him arrested. Now, that she knew she had to deal with the issue of keeping their relationship a secret from the Joneses and inadvertently involving Jeremiah in a lie, she was a pure bundle of nerves. She knew all too well how important honesty was to Jeremiah. They had had many discussions on the topic that long ago summer. Jeremiah had declared, emphatically, that honesty was the most important trait he looked for in a person. Bianca had claimed that honesty was pretty high on her list, too, although loyalty and responsibility battled for first. What must he think of her now?

If she were honest with herself, Bianca had to admit that part of her current angst lay in her fears that Jeremiah would confront her about their past, and she'd have to admit to him that she'd run away from him and an anticipated marriage proposal because she'd been afraid. Afraid that the love he promised couldn't have been genuine. After all, if her parents could divorce after being together for a quarter of a century, what chance could she have had with someone she'd just met? Bianca was so caught up in her own thoughts she did not realize that Jeremiah's eyes had been riveted on her for most of the drive back to Marissa and Steve's home.

*****

Jeremiah had been watching Bianca ever since she'd come out of Mrs. Jones's house. She hadn't said anything, but it was evident she was upset. Her rigid back and tight grip on the steering wheel were dead giveaways. That and the fact that she'd not even glanced in his direction. Jeremiah knew Bianca was upset, but how could she be upset when she'd been the one who'd turned away from their love? He wished he knew exactly what was going through her mind.

He felt so stupid! In that moment when Mrs. Jones had asked him how he felt about Bianca, he'd realized he'd not only loved her ten years ago. He loved her still. How could Bianca mean so much to him, and Mrs. Jones never even knew they'd been dating? He and Bianca had spent practically all of their free time together after they'd completed their respective internship hours, him in corporate

America, and Bianca at Reverend Jones's church. Surely, Reverend and Mrs. Jones had seen… Wait a minute!…Bianca and Marissa had always met him and Steve somewhere other than Marissa's house? No wait! … He'd always met the three of them somewhere other than Marissa's house. Restaurants… Steve's apartment… someone else's home… but not once at Marissa's house. How had he missed that? How had it never dawned on him that he'd always met Bianca, Steve, and Marissa somewhere other than Marissa's house?

When he'd sabotaged his truck prior to ringing Mrs. Jones's doorbell, he'd been planning to confront Bianca about driving to Mrs. Jones's home without him. He'd already assumed Bianca wasn't ready to talk about their past, and he hadn't planned to force her to do that. But now…Jeremiah wasn't even sure where to start. Had their relationship not meant anything to Bianca? Could he have been that blind? He had to know.

After Bianca had given that damn letter to Marissa to deliver to him, she'd basically removed herself from his life. He'd called her at least a dozen times trying to find out what had happened. She'd never answered her phone. And she'd never returned his calls even though he'd left several long, detailed messages asking her to call him so they could talk about what had happened between them. Had their relationship been part of an act? Jeremiah refused to believe that it had been.

Jeremiah loved Mrs. Jones and respected her as his elder. He didn't like having to pretend that he'd just met Bianca a couple days ago. He'd gone along with the ruse to protect Bianca in the moment, but he had no intention of continuing that lie. His parents had taught him and his siblings that once you told one lie, you had to keep telling lies to cover that first lie until you no longer knew what the truth was.

Jeremiah was determined to get to the bottom of things. His main problem, though, was how to do that without adding more hurt on top of what Bianca had recently experienced with her ex-fiancé. The last thing he wanted to do was to push Bianca further away.

When he'd read Bianca's note telling him that she'd gone to Mrs. Jones's house without him, "…to help Mrs. Jones," he'd made up his mind right then and there that they would not return home in separate cars. He'd decided he wouldn't give Bianca the option of avoiding him when he had her this close. Not this time. Now…first, he was determined to find out why the Joneses never knew about their relationship. Then…he was determined to find out why Bianca had run from him all those years ago.

After he got the answers to his questions, he'd decide his next steps. If they were going to cohabitate for the next couple of weeks, he needed to know that Bianca hadn't been laughing at him behind his back all those years ago. If he didn't like the answers she gave him, he'd find somewhere else to stay until Bianca left. He'd just have to deal with Steve.

~~~~~

CHAPTER FOUR

Jeremiah waited until Bianca had pulled into Steve and Marissa's garage, turned off the engine and pushed the button to close the overhead door before confronting her. Even as angry as he was, he hadn't wanted to be the cause of Bianca having an accident. He just needed answers to his questions.

"Can you tell me what just happened back there?" He demanded turning to face Bianca. "Why did Mrs. Jones not know about our relationship that summer? Was it all a game to you and Marissa? Did you two have a bet or something about who could make the biggest fool out of her guy? Marissa married her guy, so I can't imagine she was in on it. Was it a Chicago thing or something? Who can find a country bumpkin and bump his head?" Jeremiah had meant to remain calm, but obviously, he was not controlling his emotions very well.

"You cannot possibly believe a word of what you just said!" Bianca exclaimed more loudly than she preferred as she turned to face Jeremiah, horrified that he could actually believe any part of what he'd just said. "How can you think my feelings for you were not real? How can you think what we had was all a game?" Even with her vivid imagination, Bianca hadn't conjured up the idea that Jeremiah would think she'd misled him or played a game with his emotions.

"I have no idea what to think! All I know is you were here and then you weren't. You gave Marissa that damn Dear John letter …some BS about '…what we had couldn't possibly be real' You never answered my calls or called me back. Now I find out Mrs. Jones never even knew we were dating. What in the hell was that about?" Even as he finished the statement, Jeremiah realized he was probably a bit over the top. It might've been the look on Bianca's face, but he could also hear his own tone and volume. Jeremiah forced himself to take a few deep breaths to calm down.

"Jeremiah, it might sound stupid now," Bianca stated after what seemed like an eternity to Jeremiah, "but Jesus Christ! We were nineteen! Marissa was a preacher's daughter, and I was visiting the Joneses for the second time. We were pretty sure that Marissa's parents would not have understood that wild child from Chicago-- that den of sin--whom they'd welcomed into their home had come all the way to Houston and fallen head-over-heels in love with a guy I'd just met. So we just conveniently made sure they never knew. I am so sorry you thought any of that was about you. Jesus Christ!" Holding her tears at bay, Bianca-- determined that Jeremiah would not see her bawling like a fool—exited the car at a run not stopping until she'd enclosed herself in the guest bathroom punctuating the sanctity of her refuge by slamming the door.

Caught off guard Jeremiah sat in his seat trying to figure out what to do next. Why did women have to cry? Didn't they know what it did to men? The last thing he'd meant to do was make Bianca cry. Jesus…He'd learned as a teenager with his sisters that making women cry never ended up being as much fun as he'd anticipated in the long run. Since entering adulthood, he'd put special effort into avoiding making women cry. In spite of his turmoil, though, Jeremiah had to admit, he'd gotten an answer to at least one of his questions. The way things were going, it didn't look like he was going to get the answer to his second question any time soon, but if Bianca had really been in love with him ten years ago, there was a possibility that she still had some feelings for him. As Jeremiah saw it, all was not lost.

*****

Bianca slammed the bathroom door while simultaneously releasing the breath she hadn't realized she was holding. What in the heck had she gotten herself into? How in the world could Jeremiah believe those awful things about her? How could he have not known that her love for him was real? From the first time they'd met, she'd been drawn to Jeremiah. Her attraction to him had been instantaneous and almost magical. And now, Jeremiah thought it had all been part of some sort of game. One of her greatest pet peeves was people who purposely hurt others. And now, Jeremiah thought she'd done just that to him.

Leaning on the vanity, Bianca silently let her tears flow into the sink while she fought for the inner strength to deal with the matter at hand: Jeremiah's misconceptions and her long overdue apology to him. As she contemplated the issue, Bianca realized she'd never answered Jeremiah's second question. How could she tell him why she'd left without revealing the insecurities she had worked so hard to cover up by throwing herself into her education?

During high school, she'd never kept a boyfriend because she wouldn't "go all the way" when it seemed everyone else was doing just that. She'd been so focused on preparing for her career as a teacher, and ultimately a college professor, that she'd avoided anything that might keep her from achieving her goals. She hadn't wanted to end up like her classmates who'd ended up pregnant and out of options.

After a few repeats of that scenario, the last her freshman year of college, Bianca had given up all pretense of dating and concentrated on her studies. Her summer with Jeremiah had been so unexpected, she didn't even count that as dating. That had been just a pure magical period in her life. When she'd returned to school that fall, everything had been business as usual with her head buried in her books. The next time Bianca had even thought about dating had been during graduate school when she'd met David at a networking event hosted by the university.

Bianca's sisters hadn't seemed to have the same problems she'd experienced. Both were happily married now, but in high school, they'd both dated any number of guys and had mastered the art of flirtation. When they'd gotten together, the twins would put their heads together, giggling and flat out laughing about each other's escapades. Bianca had always felt like an outsider. Whatever "it" was that drew males to her sisters like bees to honey, she was obviously missing.

Bianca had only entered into her relationship with David as a chance to prove herself wrong. They'd dated for six months before she'd become physically intimate with him. Bianca had just felt that it was time. She'd begun to sense that if she hadn't given in soon, he'd be in the wind like her high school boyfriends. She'd loved David, but she just hadn't felt physically drawn to him as she'd remembered feeling with Jeremiah years earlier. When Jeremiah had even lightly touched her, Bianca had felt she would burst from the contact. It had been like everything she had read about in the romance novels she loved so much but had never experienced firsthand. Jeremiah had never pushed her for more. They'd just enjoyed one another's company and episodes of serious necking. Bianca had attributed that to the fact that he'd been older, and therefore more mature than the previous males she'd dated.

She and Jeremiah had spent almost every free moment together that summer. Although she'd enjoyed the time she spent teaching the children in the church summer academic camp, each day she'd looked forward to the end of the day when she and Jeremiah would meet up at whatever place had been designated. Jeremiah had also been completing an internship, but his was with an international business firm. He'd been preparing for his first year in Harvard's MBA program. Their whole relationship had played out like a dream from the moment Steve had introduced them. The two of them had even begun to talk about the oh-so-illusive future as if they would be together in it.

When Bianca's mom had called her to tell her that she and Bianca's dad were getting a divorce after twenty-five years of marriage, Bianca had been shattered. Even though her mom had been talking about her parents' situation, all of the fears and self-doubts about her ability to maintain a relationship with a man had surfaced causing Bianca to go into a tailspin. In no time at all, the conversation had become no longer about Bianca's parents. All those scenarios with ex-boyfriends dumping her had flashed before her eyes, playing like a continuous video loop, convincing Bianca that she'd been living in a magical bubble that needed bursting. Right then and there, Bianca had decided that for once she was going to be the one who removed herself from the equation before she could be dumped.

Until then, she and Jeremiah had only been able to spend stolen hours together in the evenings and on weekends. Now that the summer camp had officially ended and Jeremiah had also completed his internship, they'd be able to spend more time together before she had to return to Chicago. Once that happened, Jeremiah would see all of her flaws that her previous mates had seen, and ultimately, he'd also dump her. Bianca knew that she wouldn't be able to handle being dumped by Jeremiah. She'd been able to deal with her previous boyfriends dumping her because she'd not been in love with them. Her heart simply hadn't been invested in those relationships.

However, with Jeremiah, she had slowly, but surely, fallen head-over-heels in love.

Bianca had run from Jeremiah to prevent from being dumped, yet again. Even his numerous voicemail messages had failed to convince her to re-think the possibility that what they'd shared was real and lasting. Now, Bianca was devastated to think that Jeremiah had thought those awful things about her. She had never meant to cause him such pain. In fact, she'd always felt guilty for running away like she'd done. Bianca knew that she was not going to be able to put her long overdue apology off for much longer. If only Jeremiah would give her a little more time, she'd come clean and own up to why she'd left ten years ago. Doing that meant she would have to bare her soul and give voice to the many self-doubts and feelings of lack that had pervaded her childhood. Her parents' divorce had only wakened her deepest fear—that she was not worthy of love. How she would bring herself to share those details with Jeremiah, Bianca was not sure, but she would if it would remove that haunted and dejected look from his eyes. She owed him that much.

*****

After convincing himself that there was still hope for Bianca and him, Jeremiah exited the car with a new lease on life. He would give Bianca time to calm down, and then he'd figure out a way to get her back into his life. He wasn't against flying by the seat of his pants if it would get Bianca back into his life, but he preferred to work with a plan. Since the two of them were going to be at Steve and Marissa's house together, anyway, they could just use that time to get reacquainted with one another. Surely, she'd see they belonged together. When Jeremiah entered the house, he went looking for Bianca hoping they could continue the conversation. Admittedly, they both were upset, but he had confidence that they could work through the situation. In retrospect, everything Bianca had said made sense. She and Marissa had been nineteen. And Marissa had been a preacher's daughter. Even though, he'd been a kind, loving man, Reverend Jones had always depicted a stern, no nonsense persona. Jeremiah chuckled when he thought about what Bianca had said about Chicago being a "den of sin." He was going to have to ask her about that. He wasn't sure where that had come from, but Bianca had been the epitome of grace and prudence when they'd met. How anyone could have thought of her as a product of a "den of sin" was beyond Jeremiah.

When Jeremiah came upon the closed bathroom door, his first thought was that maybe the situation needed a little more time than he'd initially thought. Having grown up with two sisters and a cousin who spent many summers with his family, Jeremiah, knew that the bathroom often served as a haven for women. Although his sister Alexandria had once spent an entire night in the bathroom—later she'd said she was trying to make a point—he didn't expect that Bianca would resort to such tactics. He would just wait patiently for her to exit on her own. In the meantime, he set about preparing them both cups of herbal tea. He was definitely a coffee man, but if it would help the situation, he would endure a cup of herbal tea. His mom and sisters swore chamomile worked wonders at calming nerves. Marissa obviously believed the same thing because she kept a stash on hand and Jeremiah had often sat with her and Steve while she drank tea before retiring for the night. Lord knew he definitely needed something to calm his nerves now.

When the teapot began to whistle and Bianca had not emerged from her haven, Jeremiah turned off the fire and knocked lightly on the bathroom door. When Bianca didn't respond immediately, he knocked again a little harder.

"I'll be out in a minute." Bianca responded calmly having cemented her plan of action in her head. Turning on the sink faucet, she let the water run until it was hot before she wet her face cloth and washed her face as if that were the reason she'd gone into the bathroom in the first place. The last thing she did before leaving the guest bathroom was to wet her face cloth again, this time with cold water, and hold it over her eyes for a two full minutes hoping to decrease any puffiness that might have developed from her crying spell. Just before she turned the doorknob, it occurred to Bianca that if she had sequestered herself in the den while she regrouped, she might've been able to prolong the remainder of her conversation with Jeremiah until the next morning. Unfortunately, she couldn't hide in the bathroom all night long.

*****

Jeremiah backed away from the door, but only enough to let Bianca out when she opened the door. As soon as she exited the bathroom, he looked pointedly at her trying to get a read on her mood. He knew that she'd washed her face because the eye shadow and lip gloss she'd worn during dinner with Mrs. Jones were gone. The slight puffiness of her eyelids confirmed his belief that she'd indeed been crying, but she seemed to be fine now. Jeremiah wanted desperately to take Bianca into his arms, but he sensed that was not what she needed or wanted right now.

"I made hot water for tea if you'd like some. I thought we could drink it while we talk. I am so sorry I was so upset in the car. I didn't mean to yell at you. I was just so upset when Mrs. Jones made that statement about being surprised we hadn't met over the years. Man! All kinds of thoughts started going through my head." Jeremiah stated as calmly as he could muster.

"I am so sorry, Jeremiah. I had no idea you didn't know that Reverend and Mrs. Jones didn't know we were seeing each other that summer. I promise you I never meant to hurt you." Bianca responded looking directly into Jeremiah's eyes fighting back the tears that formed in her own as she spoke.

The tears glistening in Bianca's eyes, were Jeremiah's undoing, and he no longer had the control to resist pulling her into his arms. He took one step forward closing the short gap between them and wrapped his arms around her lightly. For a moment, she just stood still with her arms at her sides, but then she wrapped her arms around his waist and laid her head on his shoulder.

Jeremiah wished they could maintain that position forever. He wanted to pull her close enough to him so that he could take in her scents, but he didn't risk Bianca pulling away from him. This wasn't exactly what he'd had in mind when he'd thought about holding Bianca in his arms again, but for now, he'd rejoice in even this contact. At least she hadn't pushed him away.

Bianca didn't know what had possessed her to wrap her arms around Jeremiah or to rest her head on his shoulder. All she knew was that when he'd taken that step toward her and pulled her to him, she'd felt like she'd come home. Until that moment, she'd not realized how much she had missed Jeremiah and the constant physical contact they'd shared even though sexually, they'd never done more than heavy necking. Whenever they'd been together, they'd always touched one another exchanging what her mom would have called love pats.

Bianca expected that Jeremiah was just as surprised as she by the turn of events. After a few minutes of savoring his embrace, she decided she'd better take control of the situation or she'd not be able to pull herself away from Jeremiah unscathed.

"I don't know about you, but I prefer my tea hot," she stated simultaneous raising her head and removing her arms from around Jeremiah's waist before stepping back. She'd decided that humor might be the safest way to defuse the tension in the air. "Do you like yours with sugar or sugar substitutes?" She continued while walking to the kitchen and removing cups and saucers from the cabinet and setting them on the table.

With her peripheral vision, Bianca acknowledged that Jeremiah had remained in the same spot for a few seconds after she'd walked away. She wondered if he were hesitant in anticipation of what she might say, or if the brief contact during their embrace had sent him down memory lane as it had done for her.

Purposely, Bianca placed Jeremiah's cup and saucer at the head of the table and hers to his left to avoid awkward moments such as the one that had occurred at breakfast her first day in town when they'd been seated across from one another. She was not ready for the intensity of his gaze when she told him what was on her mind.

"What flavor do you prefer?" Bianca asked removing boxes of herbal tea from the cabinet and setting them on the counter. "I'm having apple cinnamon," she stated while placing a tea bag in the cup directly in front of her.

"I'll have whatever you're having," Jeremiah responded, determined to let Bianca take the lead in their conversation. Having watched Bianca closely from the time she'd exited the bathroom, he could tell that she was upset about more than what he'd asked her in the car. He had no intention of sending her running to the bathroom again. Nor did he want to be responsible for putting any more tears in her eyes.

Before claiming his seat at the head of the table, Jeremiah poured hot water in both their cups. He continued to watch quietly as Bianca placed a tea bag in his cup, passed him the sugar dish, added sugar substitute to her cup, stirred her tea and took a sip that was obviously too hot.

All the elaborate plans Bianca had made in the bathroom for moving forward seemed to evaporate beneath the intensity of

Jeremiah's gaze. All of a sudden, she knew that she had to be honest with him about her feelings ten years ago. Once everything was out in the open, they could work out the details later. They also had to deal with how they were going to rectify things with Mrs. Jones. Bianca hated the situation she'd put both of them in with that one unspoken lie. And last, but not least, they had to figure out how they were going to cohabitate for whatever time remained before Marissa and Steve returned home.

After what seemed like an interminable amount of time to Jeremiah during which they both stirred and sipped tea, Bianca set her cup in her saucer and spoke slowly enunciating each word. "Once again, I am so sorry that we didn't let the Joneses know that we were dating all those years ago. Marissa and I just didn't want to cause any problems with them. She is a preacher's daughter."

Bianca watched Jeremiah intently to gage his response before continuing. It was clear to her that he accepted her explanation for why Marissa and she had kept their relationship from Marissa's parents, but it was equally apparent that he was still waiting to hear more. Bianca had no doubts he was waiting to hear the answer to the other question he'd asked her.

"Jeremiah, the truth is…" she started and then paused again before continuing. "The truth is…I was crazy about you when I met you. In fact, I was so crazy about you that the whole situation terrified me."

Jeremiah wasn't sure what he'd expected Bianca to say, but it certainly wasn't what she'd said. That just went to show him how impossible it was to understand what went on in the minds of women.

"So, let me get this straight," he responded clearly trying to make sense of what he'd heard. 'You were crazy about me, so you wrote me that Dear John letter, ran back to Chicago, wouldn't take any of my calls or call me back, and basically just disappeared.' Am I getting this right?"

"You make it sound stupid when you say it like that."

The look on his face told Bianca, that indeed Jeremiah thought what she'd said sounded like utter nonsense. In retrospect, she was not sure how she'd expected him to respond to what she'd said. However, she certainly felt that a weight had been removed from her shoulders now that she'd come clean about her feelings for Jeremiah.

She'd purposely played her feelings down a bit the second time around. Telling Jeremiah she'd been crazy about him sounded much tamer than "falling head over heels in love" with him. Maybe he'd been so upset in the car he hadn't actually heard that part of what she'd said.

Just when Bianca thought Jeremiah was not going to say anything else on the topic, he asked the million-dollar question.

"So now what?"

"Well, I guess you accept my apology, and we move on from there." Bianca answered his question as nonchalantly as possible. When Jeremiah just looked at her without responding, she continued. "We do what we can to get along so we don't end up causing problems for Marissa or Steve. And...we figure out how we're going to tell Mrs. Jones that we already knew each other without having her become upset with us."

Bianca's next steps were not exactly the one's Jeremiah had in mind, but knowing what he now knew about her feelings for him ten years ago, Jeremiah was willing to let her hold the reins a little longer. He could afford to be patient if it would help him to achieve his ultimate goal. He wanted Bianca in his life again, permanently.

"Bianca, ...I have one question" Jeremiah added purposely changing the tone of their conversation. "Reverend Jones didn't really call Chicago a 'den of sin,' did he?"

Bianca laughed out loud releasing the tension she'd felt building in her shoulders and neck in anticipation of how Jeremiah would respond to her answer to his question. "No, it wasn't Reverend Jones who called Chicago a 'den of sin.' It was one of the deacons at the church. The funny thing is I didn't know anything about that until he came up to me to apologize while I was completing my internship." Bianca went on to tell the story of the deacon stopping her in the hallway to tell her that he'd voted against a person from Chicago being selected for one of the internship positions because he'd felt the person would corrupt the youth. After meeting Bianca and hearing the students and teachers rant and rave about how great she was with the children, the deacon had felt he owed her an apology and an official welcome to the church.

~~~~~

47

CHAPTER FIVE

It was only the middle of the third day since Bianca and Jeremiah had shared what she'd begun to think of as "the talk," but from what Bianca could tell, things seemed to be working out between the two of them. Although Bianca hated that she'd caused the episode that had initiated the discussion, she was glad that she and Jeremiah had cleared the air about their past and could move on. Although Jeremiah hadn't looked like he would accept her suggestion of what they'd do next, he'd acquiesced or at least settled. Basically, they'd talked and agreed to get along for Marissa and Steve's sake as neither of them wanted to be the cause of marital problems between her friend and his cousin. Surely, it couldn't be more than another week or two before the couple returned from Paris. As long as she and Jeremiah kept things cordial between the two of them, they should be fine. The only thing they'd not discussed fully was how to deal with the matter of Mrs. Jones and how to come clean with her. Well that and the details related to what had terrified Bianca and had caused her to hightail it home and to hide from Jeremiah. If Bianca had her way, Jeremiah would never know those specific details. It was best that Jeremiah remember her the way he'd seen her ten years ago. No need for Bianca to reveal to Jeremiah that underneath the façade she exhibited, she had nothing to offer a man.

Bianca and Jeremiah had agreed that they'd take turns having the kitchen first for breakfast, lunch, and dinner in order that they'd not get in each other's space. They'd even worked out a schedule for when they'd use the family room. Bianca, in her efficient manner, had even typed out a schedule on her computer and posted it on the refrigerator. Jeremiah had suggested that they just take turns cooking but eat together, but Bianca was not having any of that. The excuse she'd offered was that since Jeremiah had been staying there by himself before she'd arrived, she didn't want to intrude on his space.

She'd also shared that when she was writing, she could produce more if she were alone. She could not have told Jeremiah that he made her uncomfortable because as long as he was around, she couldn't keep her mind from wandering and wondering what it would be like to be held by him or kissed by him again or anything of that nature.

Bianca couldn't even believe her mind was going down that path on its own now. She was the one who'd let Jeremiah go ten years ago. It wasn't even right for her to still be holding on to feelings from a decade ago. After she'd left Houston at the end of that summer, Bianca had convinced herself that what she and Jeremiah had felt for one another had been mere infatuation at the most. But now she considered the possibility that Jeremiah had been in love with her, and that she'd let a good thing go. In her honesty to herself, Bianca had to admit that clearly her feelings for Jeremiah were stronger than infatuation even after all these years had passed.

Today, it was Bianca's turn to use the kitchen for lunch, so she was revising a chapter of her manuscript while eating a grilled cheese sandwich when the phone rang. She could tell by the caller ID that it was Mrs. Jones, so she answered the phone when normally she would've let the call go to the answering machine.

"Hi, Mrs. Jones. How are you? Calm down, Mrs. Jones, I can't understand what you're saying." Bianca spoke slowly into the receiver trying to calm Mrs. Jones with her voice. Once Mrs. Jones slowed down enough so that Bianca could understand what she was saying, Bianca told Mrs. Jones that she'd be right over. Apparently, Mrs. Jones had found a litter of kittens in her yard, and one of the kittens had climbed up a tree and wouldn't come down. Mrs. Jones was worried that the kitten would hurt itself.

As Bianca drove into Mrs. Jones's driveway, she could see Mrs. Jones standing on a ladder trying to coax the kitten to come to her. Bianca quickly joined Mrs. Jones at the ladder. "Mrs. Jones, you come on down and let me get the kitten." Bianca couldn't imagine having to explain to Marissa that her mother had fallen from a ladder while Bianca had watched from the ground.

"Okay, Bianca. If you think you can get the little fella, come on. I'm just worried that he's going to end up on the garage, and then we'll really be in trouble. See he keeps heading toward that branch that overlooks the garage?"

Bianca looked in the direction that Mrs. Jones indicated as Mrs.

Jones descended the ladder, and Bianca did indeed see that the kitten seemed to be heading toward the garage. Hopefully, she could get him to come down before he got the notion to go further away from where they stood at the trunk of the tree. "Mrs. Jones, what are you using to get him to come to you? Do you have some cat food, or something?

"No, Bianca. I didn't even think of that. I've just been trying to get him to respond to my voice. But I may have some tuna or sardines in the house. Let me go in and check."

While Mrs. Jones returned to the house for something aromatic to entice the kitten with, Bianca began talking to it with soothing words. The kitten sat about a foot and a half from where Bianca could reach from the step below the top rung of the ladder, and that was as far as she felt comfortable climbing. The kitten looked at her, and she could tell the kitten was listening because of its twitching ears. Bianca surmised that the kitten was frightened because it shook like a leaf in the wind. After a few minutes, Mrs. Jones returned with a small plastic container of sardines which she handed up to Bianca. Bianca removed one of the sardines from the container and placed it as far out on the branch as she could reach. The kitten sniffed in the direction of the sardine, and tentatively began moving toward the sardine.

KaPow!!! A loud blast disrupted the quiet, startling Bianca, Mrs. Jones, and the kitten who'd reached the half-way point in route to the sardine. The kitten stopped, turned around, ran across the tree branch, and jumped onto the garage roof before Bianca had even identified the source of the noise.

"Oh, drat!" Mrs. Jones exclaimed. "That's nothing but Mr. Paul's car backfiring again. I don't know why he doesn't get that thing fixed. Look!" Mrs. Jones nodded toward the roof of her garage. "That's exactly what I was worried about. Now I don't know how we're going to get the kitten down from there."

As her heart slowed down to a normal pace, Bianca shook her head and assured Mrs. Jones that it would be okay. She would just move the ladder to the garage and climb up to get the kitten. The kitten had climbed from the tree onto the garage roof and then run to the peak of the roof apparently running out of steam. The kitten now sat shivering even more than it had before blinking its eyes as they darted back and forth rapidly as if they were trying to take in everything in its surroundings. From Bianca's perspective, the kitten appeared even more afraid than it had seemed when it had been in the tree. She'd read accounts of how frightened animals had attacked humans in response to their fear. But surely, this tiny kitten couldn't do much harm to a woman her size.

After climbing onto the roof, it occurred to Bianca that she had no idea what had possessed her to leave the ladder to go after the kitten knowing her fear of heights. Well, she didn't actually have a fear of heights so much as a fear of climbing down from heights. She'd followed her male friends and cousins up many a tree or wall during her youth, but going back down had always presented a problem for which she'd endured no end of teasing. Upon appraising the situation, Bianca felt that the safest way to get the kitten was to lie down on the slanted roof, inch her way toward it, and scoop the kitten to her chest with one hand. That way, she could use her other hand to balance herself if necessary. If the kitten remained where it was, everything should work out just perfectly.

Much to Bianca's relief, the kitten safety gods were aligned in her favor, and in just a few seconds, she had the kitten close to her bosom and was inching her way back toward the ladder.

*****

As Jeremiah walked through his new home with the construction engineer answering questions regarding the finishing touches and requesting changes to what had already been completed, his mind automatically drew up images of Bianca. It had never occurred to him when he'd hired an architect to draw up the plans for his home from his own crude drawings that he'd actually included details he and Bianca had discussed that summer ten years ago when they'd shared what they thought a dream home would look like. Now it was obvious. He couldn't wait to show Bianca what they'd created together. But he couldn't figure out how that was going to happen with her purposely avoiding him as she'd done after first admitting that she'd been in love with him ten years ago. And not just in love with him, but "head-over-heels" in love with him.

She'd tried to tone it down later when she'd said she'd been "crazy about him," but Jeremiah had heard what he'd needed to hear and latched on to that with everything he had. If Bianca still had any of those feelings left for him, Jeremiah planned to feed those flames and rekindle what they'd had. He had a good idea that all of that business she'd offered about sharing the common living areas to give him his space was just malarkey. She was hiding something. And he was as determined to find out what that something was as he was determined to get Bianca back into his life.

Jeremiah had just finished meeting with the construction engineer and had returned to his truck when he saw that he had two new voicemail messages on his phone from Mrs. Jones. Jeremiah immediately became alarmed because Mrs. Jones had had his cell phone number since he'd moved in with Steve and Marissa three months ago, and she'd never called him. He knew that if she was calling now, something must've happened either to her or to Bianca. Other than that, he couldn't understand why Mrs. Jones would call him. Jeremiah played the messages three times, but he couldn't make out the details of either of them. The first message was something about a kitten, but in the second one, Mrs. Jones's emotional status was bumped up several notches, and all he could get out of it of was something about a kitten, Bianca, and a roof. Jeremiah figured he would waste less time if he just drove straight to Mrs. Jones's house rather than trying to call her back to get clarification.

Just shy of fifteen minutes later, Jeremiah was turning down Mrs. Jones's street when he spotted Bianca lying on the roof of Mrs. Jones's garage. Immediately his heart felt like it had jumped into his throat. What in the hell was Bianca doing on Mrs. Jones's garage roof? As Jeremiah got closer to the house, he could see that Bianca held something in her left arm hugged closely to her body. Jeremiah assumed it must be the kitten that had Mrs. Jones upset in the first message she'd left. What Jeremiah couldn't figure out was why Bianca had climbed onto the roof of the garage. Didn't she realize how dangerous that was? If she fell and hurt herself, he was going to kill her himself.

As Jeremiah pulled into the driveway behind Marissa's car which Bianca had been driving during her visit, he could see Bianca inching her way on her belly toward what appeared to be a relic of a wooden ladder propped against the garage. Mrs. Jones held onto the ladder apparently in preparation for Bianca's descent. Jeremiah was confident that Mrs. Jones was nowhere near strong enough to keep Bianca from falling should the ladder give way, so he quickly exited his car and instructed Mrs. Jones to let him take the ladder. Once

Bianca got safely on the ground, he planned to ream her out for doing something so dangerous. She could be killed or at the least hurt herself badly if she fell.

It seemed to take forever, but eventually, Bianca's foot reached the top of the ladder. Without realizing it, Jeremiah held his breath as he watched Bianca gain a foothold and begin climbing down the ladder holding onto it with her right hand while using her left hand to secure the rescued kitten. With each step, the ladder wobbled beneath Bianca's weight. The fact that it did, was truly a testimony to its aged condition for Bianca could not possibly weigh that much. She looked to be about the same size as one of his twin sisters who Jeremiah knew wore a size eight.

Just when Jeremiah thought the ladder would serve its purpose for what he had determined was its last job, Bianca put her weight on one of the rungs, and it broke away from the rail making her lose her footing and slide down the ladder toward the ground which was still a good four feet away. Jeremiah quickly changed his position so that he could keep Bianca from falling or at the least to brace her fall with his body. The next thing Jeremiah knew, Bianca, the kitten and Mrs. Jones all seemed to scream at the same time, and he found himself on the ground with Bianca on top of him.

"Are you two okay?" Mrs. Jones asked quickly approaching the two of them. She pried the kitten's claws from Bianca's blouse and gently placed the kitten in a box she'd obviously previously prepared and set the box to the side. Mrs. Jones then helped Bianca and Jeremiah to right themselves without allowing them to move too quickly to prevent further injury.

"I'm okay. Just a little shaken up," Bianca responded first. "I think when I slipped, I must have scared that kitten even more than he was already because the next thing I knew his claws were in my chest. Jeremiah, how about you? Are you okay?" From the grimace on his face, Bianca knew even before he answered that Jeremiah was not okay.

"My...knee... Old...football...injury." As he slowly spoke, Jeremiah put both hands on his left knee which Bianca could see expanding even through his pant leg.

"Oh, my Lord! We have got to get you to the hospital, Jeremiah." Mrs. Jones cried out. I feel so bad. This is all my fault! I am going to get you some ice right now. Are you okay to sit there for a minute? I am going to call an ambulance!" Mrs. Jones quickly ran back inside the house.

"I am so sorry, Jeremiah," Bianca told him rubbing her hands on his back. "I know you were trying to keep me from falling."

"I'll..be..fine..I ..do..not ..want.. an ..ambulance," Jeremiah whispered as loudly as the excruciating pain would allow him to talk. When Mrs. Jones returned a few minutes later with an ice pack and a towel, Jeremiah informed her that he didn't need an ambulance. He proclaimed that he just needed to put ice on his knee.

"No, sir, Mr. Jeremiah! I will not rest until you go to the emergency room and have a doctor check you out. Now, I can take you, Bianca can take you, or I'm calling the ambulance. That is the part in which you have a choice!"

Jeremiah looked up at Mrs. Jones as if she'd suddenly sprouted horns. Where had this Mrs. Jones come from? Jeremiah could not believe that tiny sweet Mrs. Jones was issuing orders to him. In that moment, he felt as if he were being reprimanded by his mom.

"Yes, Ma'am," he murmured looking at Bianca silently pleading with her to take him to the hospital.

"I'll take him, Mrs. Jones. Just give me the name of the hospital, and I'll look up the directions on my iPhone," Bianca volunteered holding in the laugh that was begging to escape. She wished she had her phone with her at that moment so she could capture Jeremiah's expression right now. She was definitely going to tease him about the look on his face later.

Bianca followed the directions on her iPhone to the local hospital. She knew that Jeremiah must've been in serious pain because he didn't speak one word to her during the short drive. All Bianca could think about was how she hoped that she hadn't hurt him too badly when she'd fallen on top of him. She had practically been in Jeremiah's arms just prior to the fall, but she'd clearly landed on top of him once he hit the ground. Whatever Jeremiah needed her to do to help him recover, she would do it because he'd surely saved her from hitting the ground.

*****

Once they arrived at the hospital, Bianca parked in the emergency room drive and ran in to get someone to bring a wheelchair out to Jeremiah. She was not sure of the extent of his injury, but she didn't want him to put any weight on his left leg. The registration clerk asked Jeremiah a million questions and handed him some papers on a clipboard to complete before they called him back for the initial evaluation. Bianca wanted to go with Jeremiah, but he assured her that he'd do just fine. He explained to her that he and his brothers and sisters had spent their share of time in hospital emergency rooms over the years so he knew the drill and would be all right.

As Bianca looked around the emergency room area while she was waiting for the staff to bring Jeremiah back out, all she could think about was how glad she was that her mother couldn't see her now. If her mother had seen Bianca, she'd undoubtedly be embarrassed by the way Bianca looked. Bianca could only imagine the lecture her mom would deliver to her. Bianca couldn't count the number of times her mother had preached to Bianca and her two sisters about how they had to dress presentably at all times just in case they had to go to the hospital. Of course, Bianca had on clean underwear that was intact, but climbing the tree, crawling on the garage roof, and then falling from it had left her disheveled, to say the least. Jeremiah looked more together, but just barely.

Bianca was glad that she hadn't seen any blood on Jeremiah's clothes, but she was a bit worried about the size of Jeremiah's knee. She cringed as she thought about how quickly Jeremiah's knee had begun to swell after he'd hit the ground. Hopefully, the ice pack Mrs. Jones had given him to hold on his knee while Bianca had driven to the hospital had kept the swelling to a minimum. Again, Bianca noted that she truly owed Jeremiah for saving her from the fall. She would never forgive herself if she'd caused severe damage to his knee. She couldn't stand the thought of causing the man she loved to be hurt. She meant the man she had loved. Or did she? Was it possible that she was still in love with Jeremiah? She knew that she still had strong feelings for Jeremiah? But love? Could she still love him after ten years had passed?

"Will the party waiting for Jeremiah Davis, please report to the front desk? Will the party waiting for Jeremiah Davis, please report to the front desk?" The announcement over the intercom startled Bianca from her reverie. Quickly she ran to the front desk and identified herself as the party waiting for Jeremiah Davis. The receptionist informed Bianca that she should wait by a nearby door as a nurse was going to come and get her because Mr. Davis was going to be discharged soon. Consequently, the medical personnel needed Bianca to sign off on Jeremiah's discharge instructions.

As soon as Bianca reached the door the receptionist had indicated, the promised nurse opened the door asking if Bianca was with Mr. Davis. The nurse introduced herself as Martha, asked Bianca's name, and repeated what the receptionist had already informed Bianca about signing papers as she escorted Bianca to one of the curtained exam rooms of the emergency room.

Jeremiah was lying on the bed with his arm over his eyes when Martha opened the curtain. If it were not for the scorn on his face, Bianca would have thought he was just resting. On his left leg, he wore a brace which extended about four inches above and below his knee. An ace bandage peeked out from beneath the brace.

"Mr. Davis," Martha stated, "Ms. Jefferson is going to take you home now, but first we have to go over all of your discharge instructions so you both know what to expect. Since the doctor gave you codeine, he wants to make sure that the person taking you home is aware of everything." Once Jeremiah removed his hand from over his eyes and opened them, Martha began reading from a sheet that she later asked Bianca and Jeremiah to sign before handing Bianca the yellow copy she pulled from the back of the carbonless packet along with a prescription for pain medication.

Before she left the exam room, Martha informed Bianca and Jeremiah that someone from transportation would come with a wheelchair to transport Jeremiah to the door shortly. Martha told Bianca she could either go and get the car now, or she could wait for transportation to arrive. Bianca thanked Martha for her assistance and stated that she would wait there until the person with the wheelchair arrived.

"How are you feeling?" Bianca asked Jeremiah after Martha had left the exam room.

"I'm okay," Jeremiah responded. "I think I'll feel better when I can rest in my own bed."

"In that case, I'll drop this prescription off at a drug store on the way home and get you home as soon as possible." Bianca informed Jeremiah. It hurt to see Jeremiah in such pain.

A few minutes after Martha left the exam room, the doctor who'd examined Jeremiah entered after knocking lightly and introduced himself to Bianca. He reiterated what Martha had told them and assured Bianca that Jeremiah would be fine if he followed his discharge orders. He also instructed Bianca to make an appointment to bring Jeremiah to his office in two weeks.

Shortly after Dr. Phillips left Jeremiah and Bianca, the transportation representative arrived and assisted Jeremiah into the wheelchair before pushing him to the exit door where he indicated he'd wait for Bianca to return with the car.

Bianca was walking to Marissa's car when her cell phone rang. Expecting that the caller was Mrs. Jones, she answered the phone using her Bluetooth earpiece.

"Bianca, this is Marissa. My mom just called. What happened? She said something about you and Jeremiah falling from a ladder. Is everything okay?"

"Hey, Girl! I am okay, but Jeremiah messed up his knee." Bianca announced after recovering from her initial surprise at the identity of her caller. "Jeremiah said it was an old football injury. We're at the hospital now, and I am going to get the car to take him home. The doctor said he has to keep weight off his leg for a couple weeks, and he should be fine...Girl, we've got to talk! You will not believe what happened the other day! Jeremiah found out that your parents didn't know we'd dated all those years ago, and he had a fit!" Bianca went on to explain what had happened as quickly as possible. "Your mother is going to kill both of us when she finds out we lied to her all those years ago. Girl, it was awful! You and Steve just have to hurry up and get home!"

"I'm not worried about Mom. She'll understand. Trust me. She'll blame me more than you. I told you, when we get home, you and I are going to have a conversation about what happened between you and Jeremiah. For the life of me, I've been racking my brain trying to remember what happened that summer, and I can't think of anything that would've caused you two to go your separate ways."

Bianca winced when she thought about how she'd purposely taken advantage of Marissa's preoccupation with Steve that summer. All she'd shared with Marissa were details related to where she and Jeremiah had gone when they'd been apart from Marissa and Steve. Bianca had shared information about how much fun she'd been having with Jeremiah, but she'd never revealed the depth of her feelings for Jeremiah. Nor had she let Marissa know that she'd purposely planned her visits to Houston over the years at times when she knew there was no possibility her of running into Jeremiah. Since she'd known that Jeremiah was working at his family's trucking business in Dallas, she hadn't even considered that he could be in Houston when she'd come this time.

"I know I was busy being 'in love' with Steve, but I thought you and Jeremiah were perfect for one another," Marissa continued. "All I remember is you gave me that letter to give to Jeremiah and jetted."

"That's his version, too." Bianca replied chuckling. "But okay. We'll talk when you get home. Let me go so I can take Jeremiah home now. Take care. I love you."

"I love you, too. Stay out of trouble. Tell Jeremiah that Steve is going to call him tomorrow. I told him I'd call you today, and that we should let Jeremiah rest at least one day before we start bothering him."

As Bianca disconnected the call, she thought about Marissa's comment to her to stay out of trouble. The way things had been happening for her, trouble seemed to be following her around as if she had it on a leash. She could only wonder what would happen next.

~~~~~

CHAPTER SIX

Jeremiah wasn't sure what had woken him, but he was certain it had something to do with the vice grip on his knee. Either that or the throbbing pain that accompanied the vice grip. Maybe he should've listened to the doctor and Bianca and taken the prescription medicine after all before going to sleep. Evidently, the codeine shot the doctor administered had given him a false sense of freedom from pain. Perhaps if he just took the narcotic for the first few days, then he could start taking an over-the-counter brand pain medicine after that. The last thing Jeremiah planned to do was to ask Bianca for the prescription, but if she offered, he'd accept it. In any case, right now he had to get up to take care of personal matters. After slowly pushing himself up to a seated position, he turned his body so that his injured leg extended off the bed from the knee down. He was able to reach the crutches next to the bed and after arranging them correctly, had taken the first tentative step when Bianca startled him almost making him lose his balance.

"And just where are you going?" Bianca asked from just inside the doorway.

Jeremiah had been so focused on getting himself situated on his crutches, he'd not heard Bianca enter the suite. "To the bathroom. Where does it look like I'm going?" He responded righting himself.

"Why didn't you call me? I put that bell by your bed so you could call me." Bianca responded coming to his side to assist him.

"I can do this. Remember this is round two for me?" Jeremiah vaguely remembered Bianca telling him something about a bell before he'd fallen asleep.

"I know, Jeremiah, but Dr. Phillips doesn't want you putting any weight on that leg for at least two weeks. He told us, and that's what's written on your discharge papers. Mrs. Jones is bringing Mr. Jones's wheel chair over here later. She just wanted to clean it up before she brought it over because it's been sitting in the garage for a while." Bianca felt exasperated by not knowing exactly what to do to assist Jeremiah.

"Bianca, I am fine, but I have to get into this bathroom. I promise you I'll call you if I need your assistance. I guarantee you that I will not put any weight on this leg. My knee wouldn't let me do that even if I wanted to."

Bianca watched as Jeremiah entered the bathroom and closed the door. She straightened the covers on his bed and fluffed the pillows before realizing that she might be making Jeremiah nervous hovering in his room. She decided this might be a good time to bring him a fresh ice pack. Plus, Mrs. Jones had called a little while ago and informed Bianca that she'd be on her way back to the house soon with Jeremiah's prescription, dinner and the wheelchair.

Mrs. Jones had met Bianca and Jeremiah at the house when they'd returned from the emergency room. After helping to get Jeremiah settled into bed, she'd given Bianca the bell for Jeremiah to use when he needed her. Like the wheelchair, the bell was another item Mr. Jones had used when he'd been going through his illness.

Once again, Bianca thought about the fact that Jeremiah was hurt because of her. She was thankful that he'd tried to keep her from falling, but she felt beholden to him because he'd gotten hurt in the midst of trying to save her. Dr. Phillips had assured Bianca and Jeremiah that he'd only suffered a sprain and that implementing the home care techniques of protection, rest, ice, compression and elevation should allow time for the joint to heal and for the swelling to subside. Following the regime, which the doctor referred to as PRICE, for the next two weeks should be enough to get Jeremiah back to normal. The worst case scenario was that Jeremiah might possibly need physical therapy once the swelling subsided. It would all depend on whether or not the muscles and tendons stiffened too much from being rested during the two-week recovery period.

Bianca was filling a Ziploc bag with fresh ice when the doorbell rang. She assumed it was Mrs. Jones, but when she got to the door, she realized she'd only been half right. As promised, Mrs. Jones had returned, but she also had an elderly gentleman with her.

"Hello again, Bianca," Mrs. Jones greeted Bianca by kissing on the cheek. "What a day it has been! I asked my neighbor to follow me over here so he could put everything in his truck. Mr. Murphy, I don't know if you've met Bianca, but she and Marissa went to school together in Illinois. They've been friends forever. Bianca is like family to us. But she might not have been to visit since you moved in though."

"No, I don't think I've had the pleasure. Nice to meet you, young lady." Mr. Murphy offered his hand, and Bianca shook it.

"Mr. Murphy, if you can just bring the big stuff in, I can get the bags," Mrs. Jones stated.

"I'll help you, Mrs. Jones." Bianca offered following Mrs. Jones to the pick-up truck in the driveway. Clearly, Mrs. Jones had done more than clean off the wheelchair that had been in her garage, for the bed of the truck also contained two shower stools, a hospital bed tray, and several plastic bags marked with the name of a chain discount store.

"Mrs. Jones, we really appreciate you bringing us the wheelchair and stuff, but we didn't want you to go out spending money." Bianca stated as she brought in the last load of packages from the truck. She spoke in as nice a tone as she could muster. After all, Mrs. Jones was her elder, and she was only trying to help.

"Bianca, Jeremiah got hurt because of me and Little Trouble, so the least I could do is make sure you all have everything you need until he gets better. I just picked up a few things that should make the next two weeks easier on the both of you. I also brought a couple casseroles from the freezer so you won't have to cook if you don't feel like it. They have labels and instructions on them. And you know once the neighbors get wind that Jeremiah is hurt, they'll be bringing stuff over, too. You know how we are down here. Now help me get everything I brought for Jeremiah into in the guest suite. Then we can have dinner."

Bianca was well aware of how the Jones's neighbors responded to emergency situations. On more than a few occasions during her visits to town, she'd prepared and delivered meals and baskets, but she'd never been on the receiving end of such efforts. She expected that she'd experience Texas style good neighborliness first hand very soon.

When Bianca and Mrs. Jones entered the bedroom of the guest suite, Jeremiah was back in bed, which reminded Bianca that she'd left the ice and the pain medicine in the kitchen.

"Hi, Jeremiah, I am glad to see that you're awake. How are you feeling?" Mrs. Jones asked as she hugged and kissed Jeremiah on the check. We're going to have dinner in a few minutes. I brought soup and sandwiches from one of my favorite restaurants. I figured we'd eat light since we're eating kind of late. Do you want to eat in here or do you want to come to the kitchen?"

"Thanks, Mrs. Jones. You didn't have to go all out, but I appreciate you bringing all of this stuff here," Jeremiah responded nodding his head in the direction of the medical equipment. "It reminds me of when I hurt my knee back in college. I feel all right, but this pain is definitely kicking. If you don't mind, I am hungry, but I'd like to avoid as much movement as possible right now, so I'd like to eat sitting right here if I may. I don't want you to think I'm being anti-social or anything like that though."

"Jeremiah, I am going to bring you a fresh ice pack and pain meds right now." Bianca stated. "It is definitely, past the time you should've taken something, but I didn't want to wake you."

Bianca wasn't sure which pain medicine Jeremiah would want to take so she brought both the prescription and the over-the-counter brand back with the ice pack and a glass of water. She was pleased to see that Jeremiah took the stronger medicine. That gave her an indication that he was experiencing significant pain.

After making sure that Jeremiah was situated comfortably in front of the television with the chicken soup and Italian sandwich that Mrs. Jones had brought, Bianca and Mrs. Jones returned to the kitchen to eat.

"Mrs. Jones, I know I've already said this, but it's worth saying again. You did not have to go all out for us, but we really appreciate it." Although she hadn't wanted Mrs. Jones to inconvenience herself, Bianca was glad that she'd brought food from one of her favorite restaurants. She would have to take Mrs. Jones there one day for lunch since she had already shared that she liked it, too.

"Bianca, you and Jeremiah came to help me. It's the least I can do. Who knew that one little kitten could be the cause of so much trouble?"

"Oh, it just dawned on me that you were talking about the kitten when you said something about 'Little Trouble' before. I don't know what I was thinking. That is so apropos." Bianca responded chuckling to herself.

*****

With the women in the kitchen away from him, Jeremiah, no longer had to pretend that his knee didn't feel like it was going to explode at any given moment. When Bianca had given him a choice between the prescription and the over-the-counter pain medicine, he had chosen the former in hopes that it would work quickly and take him out of his misery. He also expected that it would put him to sleep rather quickly. That was one reason that he avoided such strong meds unless he didn't have a choice. Something about not being in control did not sit right with him.

As he ate his meal, it occurred to Jeremiah that with him needing to stay off of his leg for two weeks Bianca would no longer be able to avoid being around him. Unless she was planning on having Mrs. Jones come over every day to assist him. And Jeremiah felt he knew Bianca well enough to know that was not her plan. Bianca would worry too much about inconveniencing Mrs. Jones to ask her to come over every day. Jeremiah smiled to himself as he realized that he just might have Bianca where he wanted her. Two weeks of being together every day all day was all that it would take for her to see that Jeremiah really was the one for her, and that they belonged together. Who knew that her falling from the ladder on top of him could be the exact thing they needed to have a chance to rekindle the relationship they'd begun ten years ago.

Bianca had assured him that she'd been crazy about him ten years ago. She'd not gone into any specific details about why she'd been terrified and had run away when they'd talked after the incident at Mrs. Jones's house, but Jeremiah was certain that if Bianca had cared about him ten years ago, there had to be at least a flame left in her heart for him now. All he had to do was to help her to remember what she'd seen in him back then. Surely, he had more to offer now that he was established in his career and the family's business. After what Steve had told him about the situation with Bianca's ex-fiancé, Jeremiah didn't want to push Bianca in any way, but at the same time, he felt they deserved a chance to be together. Perhaps, if he knew more about what had scared her away all those years ago, he'd know better how to proceed.

For the second time since seeing Bianca again, Jeremiah's mind flashed back to that fatal moment ten years ago when his life as he'd known it had been shattered. As if it had happened yesterday, Jeremiah remembered going to Marissa's house to pick Bianca up for their date. That night he'd planned to propose to Bianca. Before ringing the doorbell, he'd patted the pocket of his jacket where he'd placed the platinum solitaire engagement ring he'd picked out all by himself. He'd known Bianca was "the one". His dad has always told them, "You'll know when you meet the one you want to spend the rest of your life with. The one you want to bear your children. And when you know, you'd better act on it." His dad had proposed to his mom only two weeks after they'd met. His mom hadn't accepted his dad's proposal until a year later because she'd wanted to be sure. But even she had told Jeremiah and his siblings that she'd believed their dad was "the one" from their initial meeting. Their marriage of almost forty years was a testament to true love.

When Jeremiah had rung Marissa's doorbell on that fateful day, she'd opened the door looking forlorn. "Hi, Jeremiah, I wasn't expecting to see you today. Didn't Bianca tell you she was leaving? She had a family emergency and had to cut her visit short. She didn't go into any specifics with me, but she left this morning. I thought for sure she'd talk to you. Hold on a minute, she did give me an envelope to give you."

When Marissa had returned, she'd handed Jeremiah that envelope containing the letter that had changed his life forever. In the beginning, he'd read it a million times a day trying to figure out if he'd missed something. Or to see if there was anything he could've done to prevent Bianca from leaving as she'd done. The saddest part was that neither Steve nor Marissa would give him Bianca's number in Chicago. Jeremiah understood that Steve probably didn't even have Bianca's home telephone number, but Marissa, being one of her best friends and college roommate, surely had her home telephone number. All Jeremiah had was her cell phone number, and he'd called it over and over again leaving messages, practically pleading for Bianca to call him back. Eventually, Jeremiah had continued on with his life, but he'd never gotten over Bianca. Seeing her again after all this time had to be an indication that they belonged together, especially since he now knew for sure that she had cared for him. Jeremiah knew his friends often accused him of being too positive, some even called him Polly Andy, but he didn't care. He was going to take advantage of his injury to go after what he wanted. While the women chatted over dinner, Jeremiah plotted his strategy. He wasn't against flying by the seat of his pants if it got him what he wanted.

But he preferred to work from a plan.

*****

Later that night, Bianca poured herself a tall glass of the fresh-squeezed lemonade Mrs. Jones had prepared earlier that evening and sat down in front of the television set in the family room determined to allow herself to relax before heading to bed. Jeremiah had been sleeping soundly when she'd checked on him, and she hoped he'd remain that way for at least a few hours. She'd already set the alarm on her iPhone to wake her at three and a half hour intervals so she could check on him throughout the night and give him his pain medication. The nurse had encouraged her to give Jeremiah each subsequent dose just before the four-hour time period ended to keep him well medicated at least for the first twenty-four hours. Having experienced the pain of surgery herself, Bianca was well aware of how important it was to keep the pain at bay.

All in all, what had begun as a relatively quiet day had ended as just the opposite, Bianca thought as she recalled how she'd been eating lunch and working on one of the chapters of her manuscript that afternoon when Mrs. Jones had called frantic about the litter of kittens. Bianca realized that she'd never seen the entire litter of kittens. Only Little Trouble, as Mrs. Jones had dubbed him. Bianca told herself that she'd have to ask Mrs. Jones about the rest of the litter tomorrow.

~~~~~

CHAPTER SEVEN

The next morning Jeremiah's first thought upon waking was that he felt slightly better than he had when he'd first climbed into bed after Bianca had brought him home from the hospital. Due to the fact that Bianca had woken him several times during the night, he was extremely exhausted, but he could tell that the swelling in his knee had gone down some, and thankfully, the vice grip on his knee had loosened its hold, too. Jeremiah expected that another twenty-four hours of bed rest should be all that he needed to arrive at a tolerable pain level. His re-injury vaguely reminded him of the time when he'd first torn his ACL in college. Of course, then he'd been so swamped by the ladies coming to check on him and bringing him his favorite foods that he'd not focused on his pain back then. He'd mostly thought about the pain only during and directly after the grueling physical therapy sessions he'd endured. Jeremiah hoped he would not have to go through physical therapy again. The orthopedic specialist at the hospital seemed to think that rest and ice were all he needed. But even the specialist had said that only time would tell.

As Jeremiah thought about how tired he felt, it occurred to him that Bianca had to be even more tired due to looking after him all night. Either she'd set her alarm to wake her every three or four hours, or she'd been cat napping all night. After checking the clock, Jeremiah suspected that Bianca would be in his room with another dose of medicine in less than an hour. He really wanted to take a shower and to put on clean pajamas before she came in again, but he didn't think his knee was ready to endure the level of movement a shower required. As he saw it, the best he could do at this time was to clean up in the bathroom sink until he was more able to tackle a shower. Of course, he could always ask Bianca for a sponge bath, but he didn't see that happening any time soon. He chuckled to himself as he imagined how Bianca would respond if he asked her for a sponge bath. He had no doubts that she'd blush from her forehead to the tips of her toes. With that image in his head, Jeremiah retrieved his crutches and set off to clean up and prepare for Bianca and day one of his recovery period which he also saw as day one of recovering Bianca.

*****

When Bianca's alarm went off for what felt like the millionth time, she turned it off and laid back down to collect her thoughts. She was so not a morning person, and waking several times during the night had not helped her morning disposition one bit. She made a promise to herself that once she fed Jeremiah breakfast and gave him his morning medications, she was going to take a nap. Mrs. Jones might not like that she'd miss church that day, but surely she'd understand once Bianca explained to her that she'd gotten up at three and a half hour intervals all through the night to administer Jeremiah's pain medicine.

Bianca also promised herself that after she took a nap she'd work on her manuscript. After almost a week in Houston, she'd not accomplished nearly as much as she'd hoped to have completed in that time. Once Jeremiah's pain subsided, she expected she'd be able to focus more on her writing, but for now, her first priority was helping him to heal. After all, if it had not been for him protecting her from a fall, he would not be hurt. Bianca definitely preferred looking after Jeremiah to being looked after by Jeremiah. She knew from experience that she was not a good patient. And just the thought of being looked after by Jeremiah was causing her body and mind to respond in ways that were totally unfamiliar to her. Forcing herself to wake up fully and to change the path her mind was taking, Bianca headed for the shower to begin her first full day of nursing Jeremiah back to health.

After showering, Bianca dressed in comfortable workout attire and began preparing breakfast for the two of them. Well aware that if she made carb-filled breakfasts each day, both she and Jeremiah would gain many unwanted extra pounds during his recovery period, she promised herself that she'd shop for healthy breakfast foods later that day or no later than the next day. In fact, since she'd be preparing most of their meals, she needed to shop for healthier foods, in general. She had a feeling Jeremiah would not be satisfied with the types of meals she normally prepared for herself. And she predicted that any meals sent by the neighbors were going to lean toward heavy southern cooking and not the lighter meals she'd recently begun to eat. It wasn't that she disliked heavy meals; it was more that her hips and thighs loved those meals far too much. Over the years, she'd learned to sparingly partake of the types of meals she'd grown up eating. Doing that while maintaining a regular exercise routine allowed her to maintain what she viewed as a healthy size eight. Plus, sensible eating was just plain good for her overall health. This morning she decided to prepare omelets made with half real eggs and half Eggbeaters for herself and regular omelets, turkey sausage, toast, and hash browns for Jeremiah. Although she loved potatoes cooked almost any way, she rarely allowed herself the privilege of eating them for breakfast.

While she waited for the sausage to cook and the potatoes to brown, Bianca called Mrs. Jones to give her an update on Jeremiah's progress and to let her know that she wouldn't be attending church that morning. As she had suspected, Mrs. Jones was sympathetic to her lack of sleep and even offered to come over later to look after Jeremiah so that Bianca could take a long nap. Bianca thanked Mrs. Jones for her offer but declined, assuring Mrs. Jones that she'd let her know when she needed a respite. As soon as Bianca hung up the phone, she remembered that she'd forgotten to ask Mrs. Jones about the litter of kittens. She made a mental note to ask Mrs. Jones when she came to the house after church as Mrs. Jones had promised. Bianca also reminded herself that she needed to set a time to meet with Mrs. Jones to come clean about knowing Jeremiah before this summer.

After cooking her own omelet, Bianca went to check on Jeremiah and was surprised to see him already up and dressed in clean sweats. "Well, good morning, Mr. Jeremiah. How are you this morning?"

"Good morning to you also. I would say, I am as well as can be expected. What about you after waking me up all night long although admittedly for a good cause?"

"I'd say it definitely was for a good cause. But I am exhausted as you can expect. I've promised myself that as soon as we eat breakfast, I'm going to lie back down for a bit. Mrs. Jones said she's going to come by later to check on you. She asked about you when I called her this morning. I shared with her that mostly you've been sleeping from the medicine, but you seem to be doing pretty well. She wants to 'lay eyes on you herself,' she said so she will be over later today. So are you ready for breakfast? You definitely look like it. Are you up to venturing into the kitchen, or do you want to eat in here again?"

"I think I need a change of scenery for at least a little while. I guess we'll see how well this wheelchair works."

"Good, you can keep me company while I cook your omelet. Everything else is ready."

After grabbing the wheelchair from the corner and setting the brakes, Bianca assisted Jeremiah as he moved from the bed to the chair. She could tell that Jeremiah was trying to act as if he were fine, but the clenching of his teeth and squinting of his eyes conveyed to her that each movement caused him severe pain. She winced inwardly as she once again acknowledged that she was the cause of Jeremiah's pain. She was determined to make it up to him and to make sure he recovered as quickly as possible.

Once Jeremiah was properly seated, Bianca raised the left leg rest to elevate his knee and then pushed Jeremiah into the kitchen. She thought it best to place Jeremiah at the head of the table to allow him to extend his leg beneath the table to eliminate the possibility of his knee bumping anything. The pedestal base centered beneath the table was far enough away from Jeremiah's leg to prevent it from causing a problem. All Bianca had to do was seat herself on his right side and she'd avoid coming into contact with his left leg. Once she had Jeremiah seated correctly, she poured coffee for him.

"Do you still take your coffee with two creams and two sugars?"

"I do," Jeremiah responded capturing Bianca with a piercing gaze. "I'm surprised you remember after all these years."

"Yeah, I remember quirky things," Bianca replied quickly averting her eyes as she added the cream and sugar to Jeremiah's mug. She remembered everything she'd learned about Jeremiah that summer, but he didn't need to know that. At that moment she recalled how he'd eat one forkful of each food on his plate so that he finished everything at the same time. He'd teased her about eating everything else and saving one dish until last. She'd told Jeremiah that doing that allowed her to savor her favorite foods. She'd also shared with him that her mom had always reprimanded her for eating that way.

Blocking the memory from her mind, Bianca turned toward the sink, washed her hands and sprayed oil in the pan for Jeremiah's omelet. While the eggs cooked, Bianca removed her omelet, the meat, and hash browns from the microwave oven and placed them on the table.

"Everything looks delicious, and I'm starving," Jeremiah remarked.

"That's because you didn't eat much last night."

"Yeah, I know. I was hungry, but I think the pain distracted me from eating."

After sliding Jeremiah's omelet onto his plate, and placing it in front of him, Bianca took her seat at the table.

"You did all the work. I'll say grace," Jeremiah offered reaching for her hand.

When Jeremiah's hand made contact with hers, Bianca could've sworn she felt electricity shoot up her arm and through her body. Before closing her eyes for his prayer, she quickly glanced at Jeremiah for some acknowledgement that he'd felt what she'd felt, but she detected no reaction from him.

*****

Jeremiah couldn't remember when he'd enjoyed a meal as much as he was enjoying eating breakfast with Bianca. Only it wasn't about the meal. It was about being with Bianca again. He'd been so busy being angry with her when she'd prepared breakfast for him her first day back in town that he'd not allowed himself to appreciate either the company or the food. He knew Bianca had felt the current that had passed between them when their hands had touched because he'd sensed her looking at him for signs that he'd felt the jolt right before he'd blessed the table. He'd purposely not looked in her direction, but he'd wanted to shout, "Ahah!" Bianca obviously still felt something for him. Otherwise, she'd not have felt that connection to him. And who would have thought she remembered how he took his coffee. It was only a small thing, but the fact that Bianca remembered gave him hope for their relationship.

"So, Bianca, you told me you are on a sabbatical. What exactly does that mean? I've heard the term before, but I don't really understand it."

Bianca was surprised that Jeremiah had even heard what she'd told him that first day. He'd been so obviously angry she'd not thought he'd been listening to anything she'd said. She explained to Jeremiah about her sabbatical and the manuscript she was working on based on her dissertation research. When Jeremiah asked her how she liked teaching, she shared stories about her experiences in the classroom. They laughed together about many of the escapades of her students. Bianca was pleased that Jeremiah wanted to hear about her life. In turn, Jeremiah shared stories with her about working in his family's trucking business. It really was like old times. Bianca felt herself let down her guard. Communicating openly with Jeremiah was much easier than skirting around him as she'd done since they'd talked after the dinner at Mrs. Jones's house.

After breakfast, Jeremiah wanted to go back to his bed where he could watch television, so once Bianca had him settled, she cleaned up the kitchen and then took the nap she'd promised herself. After her nap, she worked on her manuscript for a period before preparing lunch which she ate with Jeremiah in his room. Once again, Bianca relished the ease of conversation they shared while simultaneously feeling drawn to Jeremiah as she'd been that first summer. It seemed to her that Jeremiah still cared for her, and she wasn't sure how to respond to his feelings. She wasn't sure she'd be able to walk away from him again if she allowed herself to act upon the feelings she still had for him. After lunch, Bianca continued working on her manuscript until Mrs. Jones came to visit with dinner.

*****

Later that night, as Bianca prepared to get Jeremiah settled for the night so that she could do the same, it occurred to her that other than Mrs. Jones stopping by and Steve calling Jeremiah, Sunday had been a lazy day for both her and Jeremiah. So why did she feel as if she'd run a marathon? It was not as if the light lunch of soup and sandwiches or the salad she'd prepared to accompany the casserole Mrs. Jones had brought for dinner had exerted a significant amount of physical energy. The only thing she could think of that would cause her to feel so exhausted was the mental and emotional dance she'd performed while trying to maintain a safe, professional distance from Jeremiah. Safe? What an odd word to describe her relationship with Jeremiah.

Per Jeremiah's request, Bianca placed a pitcher of water by his bedside along with his prescription and over-the-counter pain pills so that he could take his own medication through the night without disturbing her. At first, Bianca had protested when he'd made his request, but seeing as how Jeremiah's pain level was lower, she had acquiesced. Jeremiah had told her that he didn't like feeling like he was being an imposition to her. She'd assured him that was not the case, but she understood how it might be difficult for Jeremiah to feel too dependent upon someone else. Had she been the one being waited on, she'd have felt the same way. She really hated to see Jeremiah just lying in bed especially knowing she was the cause of his condition. His still sleeping body was such a stark contrast to the virile energetic Jeremiah she knew.

"Okay, Mr. Jeremiah, you are good to go." Bianca announced before heading back to the den to get ready for bed herself. "Let me know if there is anything else I can do for you."

"I think I'm good. I really appreciate the way you've been taking care of me."

"Jeremiah, I told you not to thank me. You got hurt keeping me from getting hurt. Taking care of you is the least I can do."

"Bianca, there is one thing you can help me with tomorrow." Jeremiah continued. "I feel really gritty after being in this bed all day. I washed up today, but I think I'll feel well enough to take a shower tomorrow morning. But I'm pretty sure I'll need your help. Do you think you can help me take a shower in the morning?"

"What do you mean, you'll need my help?" Bianca asked shocked at his question. "How can I help?" The vision that had popped into her head was definitely not one of her helping Jeremiah take a shower.

"I'm not sure of all the particulars, but I think with the stools Mrs. Jones brought over here, I can handle everything but washing my back. So if you help me to get in the shower and wash my back, I should be fine. Are you up to that, Nurse Bianca?"

"I think Nurse Bianca is up to the task." Bianca answered Jeremiah trying to make light of his request when all she could think about was how she was going to be able to stand in a hot steamy shower washing his back without revealing to him just how much she was affected by him.

Jeremiah chuckled to himself after Bianca left the guest suite.

He had to give her credit for trying to remain calm when he'd asked her to help him with his shower, but the way her eyes had immediately gotten as big as saucers before returning to their normal size was an excellent indicator that she was not immune to him. He really did just need her help with getting in and out of the shower. He couldn't think of any reason why he wouldn't be able to wash his own back. It wasn't like when he'd torn his rotator cuff in a separate football injury than the one in which he'd injured his knee. Then he hadn't been able to reach his back and needed someone to wash it for him. No, he had made his request because he just hadn't been able to help teasing Bianca. Her facial expressions had always been so telling they never failed to amuse him.

Jeremiah knew that he'd let Bianca off the hook in the morning. He expected having her wash his back wouldn't be any easier for him than it would be for her. Even thinking about Bianca's hands lathering his back was affecting his libido. If he didn't get that picture out of his head, Jeremiah knew he'd not be able to get to sleep anytime soon. A better use of his imagination would be for him to focus on his strategy for getting Bianca back into his life for good. However, the more he thought on the matter, the more he was assured that all they needed was time and close proximity for things to occur naturally--as they had in the past--which was actually to his advantage because he despised conniving people, especially men who used their wiles to trick unsuspecting or trusting women. If he was just himself around Bianca and treated her the way his heart led him to, Bianca couldn't help but see that he still cared for her. And perhaps she'd learn to care for him again.

After leaving the guest suite, Bianca took a detour to the kitchen and tried to calm herself with a cup of Sleepy Time tea. She couldn't say exactly why Jeremiah's request had her heart palpitating, but she expected it had something to do with the intense attraction she'd felt toward him since they'd met ten years ago. After "the talk," she'd purposely avoided Jeremiah not wanting to reveal to him that even though she'd been the one to end their relationship, she'd never stopped loving him. Seeing Jeremiah after all these years only reminded her of what she'd let go. Too often through the years she'd wondered what her life would be like if she'd given in to her desires and continued her relationship with Jeremiah after that summer.

Based on the way Jeremiah had acted that night at Mrs. Jones's house and his questions afterward, Jeremiah had really cared about her. Surely, they'd have gotten married and perhaps had children by now. When they'd been together, Bianca had enjoyed the way Jeremiah had made her feel loved and protected without feeling smothered. They'd shared an easy camaraderie that most couples worked hard to achieve. It had been as if Jeremiah had appreciated her knowledge, strength, and independence and still wanted to be with her without changing who she was at the core. Bianca hadn't thought about it at the time, but it was as if they'd just clicked. Everything with them had just felt right. It fact, that feeling of rightness is what had scared Bianca the most when her mom had called with the news of her parents' impending divorce. Immediately after that call, Bianca had begun to question her judgment. How could someone she'd only known for a few weeks know her so well? And how could she know him so well in that same time period? And more importantly, how could they be sure that what they felt for one another was real and would last?

After returning first home and then back to school in Illinois, Bianca had often found her heart sending "what if" messages to her brain. Being the staunch intellectual that she was, every time one of those messages reached her brain, she'd squelch it by analyzing what had happened with her parents after twenty-five years of marriage. A marriage that Bianca certainly thought had been a happy one. Seeing Jeremiah again had only brought up possible regrets about leaving all those years ago. She'd been physically attracted to Jeremiah from the first time she'd seen him; her emotional attraction had grown during the significant time they'd spent together. Looking back on the situation, Bianca had to admit—even if only to herself—that she really had been in love with Jeremiah ten years ago. She'd told Jeremiah that she'd been 'crazy about him,' but the reality was that she'd loved him with all her heart. How she would be able to maintain her emotional distance while taking care of Jeremiah during the next couple of weeks was already a mystery to Bianca. How she could accomplish that during forced physical contact was beyond her comprehension.

Shaking her head as if to clear her thinking, Bianca finished her tea, washed her dishes and placed them in the rack to dry. She really did need to get a good night's sleep to prepare herself to help Jeremiah with his shower in the morning.

CHAPTER EIGHT

As tired as she had been when she'd gone to bed, Bianca had not slept well. It seemed every time she'd closed her eyes, visions of Jeremiah—stitch stark naked—had danced before her eyes. In one crazy dream, Jeremiah performed a stripper's dance with his towel, enticing Bianca to join him in the shower. That dream made absolutely no sense because due to the condition of Jeremiah's knee, it was impossible for him to dance like a stripper. He would be so busy keeping his weight off his injured knee he'd not be able to manipulate his body in the sexy ways he'd demonstrated during her nighttime fantasy.

Bianca silently acknowledged that it was going to be almost impossible for her to remain aloof as she rubbed a sudsy bath sponge or wash cloth up and down and across Jeremiah's back. His body had been well-developed when she'd met him ten years ago, but now, the only word she could think of to define his physical condition was buff. Even with her extensive education, more apt adjectives to describe Jeremiah eluded her at the moment. Her mind recalled precisely the muscles rippling up and down his back as Jeremiah had stood facing the police officers with his hands raised in the air the night she'd almost gotten him arrested. At the time she'd not known her prowler was Jeremiah, so she'd not permitted herself the luxury of enjoying how the muscles of his V-cut back had pointed toward the smiley faces swimming in red that caressed his tight derriere. Nor had she focused on the trunk-like thighs tapering into bulging calves. Bianca literally shuddered just remembering the view. Determined to fortify herself for the task ahead, Bianca quickly showered, brushed her teeth, and threw on workout clothes before heading to the kitchen for a cup of coffee. She was not sure how long she had to herself, but from what she'd learned so far about Jeremiah, he was a morning person, so that meant he'd be ready for her assistance shortly.

Not knowing exactly when Jeremiah would wake or how long it would take to help him with his shower, Bianca decided it made the best sense to wait until after his shower to cook breakfast. She knew she hated reheated breakfast, so she preferred not serving it to Jeremiah. After deciding on a menu of pancakes with bacon and eggs for Jeremiah and fruit and yogurt with granola for herself, she poured herself a cup of coffee. As she drank her coffee, she measured and mixed the dry ingredients for the pancakes and prepared the bacon to go into the oven. She was drinking her second cup of coffee when the sound of the bell she'd given Jeremiah alerted her of his readiness for her assistance. Bianca quickly prepared a cup of coffee for Jeremiah and took it with her to the guest suite.

When Bianca entered the guest suite, she was so surprised to see Jeremiah sitting on the side of the bed dressed in a black satin bathrobe that it took her a minute to realize that he was unwrapping the ace bandage from his knee. It had never occurred to Bianca that Jeremiah would own a bathrobe. What man his age owned a bathrobe or housecoat as her family called them? And why did he look like sex personified in what was clearly a simple piece of fabric? Quickly, Bianca clamped down on the thought running through her head that beneath the robe, Jeremiah was stitch stark naked just like he'd been in her dream.

"Jeremiah, I think you should leave the bandage on while you take your shower," Bianca stated once his actions registered through the fog of her brain. As she spoke, she placed Jeremiah's coffee on the bedside table hoping the trembling of her hand did not reveal her state of mind. "I think leaving the pressure on will keep it from swelling while you stand up."

Jeremiah paused, considering Bianca's suggestion before asking, "Do we have a second bandage to change into once this one is wet?"

"Good question. I don't think we do...I have to add that to my shopping list." Bianca responded. "I guess we'll just have to risk possible swelling. How about you leave your knee wrapped until we get you seated in the shower then?"

"That makes sense." Jeremiah responded changing the direction of his movements and re-wrapping his knee. When he'd secured the clips in the bandage, he sat up and faced Bianca. "Good morning.

How are you today? Are you ready for this?"

"Good morning to you, too. I am fine. Thanks for asking. I am as ready as I will ever be. I have never dropped a patient, and I do not plan to do that today. Go on and drink your coffee while I get the shower ready. I want to make sure the stools are in place and the water is hot before we get you in there."

Jeremiah watched Bianca as she moved around in the bathroom. He could tell she was nervous, and he'd bet her anxiety had nothing to do with dropping him and everything to do with being in the close confines of the shower with him. He had to admit to himself that he was not as calm as he wanted her to believe he was either. The open shower stall was large enough to hold a group of people, so situating the stools to accommodate one injured person should be a simple task. However, that same openness left no room for privacy. Jeremiah had often wondered why Steve and Marissa had designed the guest suite with resort-like features. The open, over-size shower stall and spa tub were just two examples of such amenities.

To date, Jeremiah had never been in a shower with someone with whom he was not physically intimate, so this experience was definitely going to be a new one for him. He would have to make sure that he kept his back to Bianca at all times to make sure she didn't witness his body's natural response to her closeness. Already, he could feel himself reacting to her as she prepared the shower for him dressed in exercise gear that covered her body and yet revealed obvious muscle definition. Jeremiah had never thought about how Bianca maintained her sleek girlish figure, but the way the spandex hugged her body gave him the distinct impression that she worked out on a regular basis. By the time his convalescence period was up, Jeremiah expected to know as much as he could about Bianca, even down to minute details such as those related to her exercise routine.

During the summer they'd dated ten years ago, Jeremiah had learned quite a bit about Bianca. He knew that she was the baby of three girls. Her older sisters were twins like his baby sisters. Her parents were high school educators, and Bianca had always wanted to follow in their footsteps in the field of education. She'd wanted to be a college professor even though she also loved teaching children. Jeremiah had witnessed her easy rapport with the elementary age children when he'd arrived early one day to pick Bianca up at Reverend Jones's church where she'd been completing her internship. Even from the short time he'd observed her bringing the lesson to a close and preparing the youngsters for dismissal, Jeremiah could see that Bianca was a natural teacher, and her students loved her.

Jeremiah also knew that Bianca loved reading, dancing, and playing board games. During their summer together, they'd often read to one another from poetry anthologies and whatever contemporary novels either one was reading. Jeremiah had been impressed that Bianca took the time to literally just enjoy reading. Too many of the young women he'd known had been so focused on beautifying themselves they hadn't indulged in the printed word. Hands down, Bianca's favorite form of physical enjoyment had been dancing. She'd taught Jeremiah all of the latest dances which they'd practiced at outings at the homes of Steve and Marissa's friends as well as at various night clubs. They'd often ended their escapades playing timeless board games like Monopoly, Sorry and Clue.

Jeremiah knew he'd not imagined the fun they'd shared or the closeness they'd developed during that three-month period. He also realized that a lot could have changed in ten years, but he was determined to catch up. And most importantly, he was determined to find out what had made Bianca run from him and from their relationship. There was no doubt in his mind that he needed to figure that out before they could move forward.

*****

Bianca could feel Jeremiah's eyes on her as she prepared the resort style shower stall for their use. She doubted that he shared any of the apprehensions she held about being in a shower stall with him. Even though she was fully dressed and would not be showering with him, Bianca was overwhelmed about the prospect of the intimacy attributed to being in such close quarters with Jeremiah. Taking showers with women was probably a normal part of his couple's routine, but Bianca had never experienced what some might have considered a simple act. Of course, the fact that they were not a couple in spite of her attraction to him, made matters even worse.

Once the stools were in place, Bianca removed both the bath rugs so that Jeremiah could maneuver the crutches easily without falling. Next, she turned on the water in the shower. The doorway was not wide enough to accommodate the wheelchair, so Jeremiah had to walk from the entrance to the bathroom to the shower. Bianca then hung the bath towel she'd taken from the linen closet on one of the hooks right outside the shower stall. When she was satisfied that the water temperature was hot enough for Jeremiah, she turned off the faucet and let him know that she was ready for him to join her.

Bianca watched as Jeremiah made his way from the entrance of the bathroom to the shower stall. With each swing forward on the crutches, his robe pulled open revealing glimpses of what surely had to be a pair of the sexiest male legs Bianca had ever seen. But then again, she wasn't in the habit of looking at the legs of almost naked men. Besides the girly magazines she and her college friends had shared, her experiences viewing men's body parts had mostly been limited to admiring the way the uniforms drew attention to the well-defined thigh and calf muscles of football and baseball players. Silently groaning, Bianca acknowledged once again that helping Jeremiah to shower was not going to be an easy task for her.

"How about you step in the stall and then hand me your robe so I can hang it on this hook. You should probably keep at least one of your crutches in the shower stall with you, too," she suggested when Jeremiah had stopped directly in front of her.

"Sounds like a plan, Nurse Bianca. No ogling me from behind." Jeremiah teased swinging into the shower and handing her first a crutch and then his robe.

"Mr. Jeremiah, I can't help you with my eyes closed. Don't tell me you're shy."

"You can bet I won't be the one blushing during this shower, lady. Don't you tempt me into pulling you in here with me," Jeremiah responded easing down onto one of the stools Bianca had placed in the stall.

"I am fully dressed," Bianca countered.

"We can remedy that pretty quickly," Jeremiah quipped placing his injured leg onto the second stool and unwrapping the ace bandage.

Too late, Bianca realized she'd allowed herself to be suckered into responding to Jeremiah exactly the way he'd wanted. She could already feel the heat rising up her neck and toward her face. Not wanting to let on to him how flustered she was, she asked, "Do you want me to wash your back now, or do you want to call me back for that?"

"I'm good." Jeremiah responded thinking it was time to let Bianca off the hook. He wasn't looking at her face, but he suspected she was turning red. "You go on and relax. I was just teasing you about washing my back."

"Jeremiah,..." Bianca began, but Jeremiah cut her off before she could complete her sentence.

"Of course, I won't complain if you insist." He chuckled as he handed her his ace bandage.

"No, I'm good. Call me when you need my help getting out. I'm going to make breakfast," Bianca announced on her way out of the bathroom after placing the ace bandage on the vanity.

Don't ogle him indeed, Bianca thought to herself as she headed to the kitchen. Any woman with blood in her veins would delight in viewing that fine specimen of man. She could've choked him for keeping her up half the night worried about how she was going to survive washing his back. She was certainly glad that Jeremiah had been teasing her, but she was determined that she'd get him back for the mental anguish he'd caused her. She remembered from their brief time together in the past that Jeremiah had taken personal delight in mocking her innocence and naiveté. He had once accused her of perpetrating being a city girl. Said he'd never known a city girl who blushed as often as she did. Bianca knew she had to definitely work on not allowing herself to respond to Jeremiah's antics.

While she prepared breakfast for Jeremiah, Bianca remembered that she'd forgotten to put Jeremiah's bell where he could access it when he was ready for her assistance. She would just have to listen carefully to hear him when he called her.

*****

With Bianca out of the bathroom, Jeremiah finally felt that he could let down his guard. He'd been purposely teasing Bianca because he really didn't want her to know that all of a sudden the bathroom he'd thought was over-size a few minutes ago had started feeling cramped. If he hadn't run Bianca out of the room, there was no telling what would've happened. He was sure that if she'd caught even a snippet of his frontal view, she'd have been astonished and possibly even frightened, and that is not the effect he was aiming for with his strategic plan to woo Bianca back into his life. No, Jeremiah was determined that he'd manage alone in the shower even though his knee had begun to throb almost as soon as he'd removed the ace bandage. Standing only as long as absolutely necessary, he completed the task of showering in no time at all before returning to a seated position on the stools to recuperate. After regaining his strength, Jeremiah stood again and finished his shower with a cool blast of cool water before calling out to Bianca to assist him again.

When Jeremiah called out to Bianca, she quickly went to him and helped him get out of the shower stall and back into his bedroom. She left him to get dressed while she returned to the kitchen to finish breakfast and to fix his plate. When Jeremiah entered the kitchen a few minutes later, Bianca was pouring him a fresh cup of coffee. He joined her at the table and once again prayed over their meal before they ate.

After breakfast, Bianca left Jeremiah watching television in the family room while she went to the store to pick up a few groceries and a second ace bandage for Jeremiah. Overall, she was pleased with the progress Jeremiah was making. He'd shared with her that his pain level had decreased, and the swelling in his knee had obviously decreased, though his knee was not yet back to its normal size. The nurse had informed them that it might take a week for all the swelling to subside. If Jeremiah's progress continued as it had started, Bianca speculated that after the prescribed two weeks of keeping weight off his knee, Jeremiah would be back to his old self.

*****

"I think you're cheating me! Let me see those directions again." Jeremiah shouted at Bianca later that afternoon as they played the board game Risk. He'd never played the game before, but Bianca had shared that it was one of her family's favorite. In fact, Jeremiah had never even heard of the darn game before Bianca had dragged it out of one of Steve and Marissa's closets. For all he cared, she could put it back where she'd found it. They'd begun playing right after Bianca had cleaned up the kitchen following lunch. And now it almost time for dinner.

"Jeremiah, stop whining! I am not cheating you," Bianca protested as she leaned in to show Jeremiah the rule as she read it aloud. For the last two hours that had been the pattern every time he'd challenged the way she was playing the game. Each time she'd gotten close to him, his cologne had permeated her senses. Why did he have to wear one of her favorite male fragrances? "I win since you don't have any more countries. Quit being a sore loser. This is your first time playing. You'll get better the more we play," she added as she began gathering the game pieces and returning them to their respective cases.

"I don't think I want to play that again," Jeremiah retorted helping her to pack the materials back into the box. "Next time we play Monopoly, and I'm going to win then. I'm the King of Monopoly."

"Jeremiah, I am not thinking about you. I'm going to start dinner. Mrs. Jones is joining us. How about after dinner, loser gets to pick the movie we watch," Bianca responded shaking her head and chuckling.

"I'll pick a movie all right. And you can bet it won't be a chick flick."

*****

Later that evening, Bianca was removing the tuna casserole from the oven when she heard Mrs. Jones pull into the driveway. "Perfect timing," she announced as she greeted Mrs. Jones with a kiss on her cheek. "What have we here?" She asked relieving Mrs. Jones of the picnic basket she held.

"Pecan pie and pineapple upside down cake."

"Mrs. Jones, you are too good to us," Bianca stated wincing from the guilt she held inside. "I'm definitely going to have to rev up my exercise routine while I'm here. Luckily, when I shopped this morning, I bought healthy food to go along with what you and the neighbors keep bringing. If I could just say 'no,' I'd be fine. Make yourself at home. The rolls will be ready in about five minutes, and then we can eat."

"Are you sure you don't need me to do anything to help?"

"No. The table is set and we're just waiting on the rolls. Jeremiah is in the guest suite, but he'll be back in here in a minute."

"Okay then. I'll just wash my hands in the guest bath."

*****

Dinner with Mrs. Jones had given Jeremiah an opportunity to observe Bianca unobtrusively. The three of them had dined on tuna casserole, salad, and yeast rolls with pecan pie and French vanilla ice cream for dessert. It was clear to Jeremiah that Bianca truly was like a daughter to Mrs. Jones. Mrs. Jones had shared snippets of stories of Marissa and Bianca from their college days as well as bits from their after college ventures.

Jeremiah had interacted with Mrs. Jones several times over the past years at family gatherings, but then she'd just been Marissa's mom and Steve's mother-in-law. Now he saw Mrs. Jones from a different perspective. She was Bianca's surrogate mother, mentor, and friend. From witnessing their relationship in action, Jeremiah could understand why it bothered Bianca so much that the two of them had not been forthcoming with the knowledge that they'd met and dated years ago. It also made sense that Marissa and Bianca would've held back that information when the girls were teenagers. For that is clearly how Mrs. Jones had viewed them back then. They were "her girls." One natural born, both God given.

Before Mrs. Jones left, she'd shared with Jeremiah and Bianca that she was scheduled to attend a women's retreat with church members the following Sunday. She had asked the two of them if they wanted her to cancel her trip in case they needed her. Jeremiah chuckled as he thought about how he and Bianca had responded almost in unison that Mrs. Jones was not to cancel her trip. Mrs. Jones had also informed them that Mr. Murphy would be looking after Little Trouble in her absence. She'd explained that the other kittens in the litter had disappeared from the spot where she'd found them in her yard. The veterinarian had hypothesized that the mother had most likely come back for her kittens and had taken the others to a safe environment while Mrs. Jones and Bianca had focused on rescuing Little Trouble. The veterinarian had also hinted that the mother could possibly still come back for Little Trouble, but since the kitten was eating on its own, the mother might merely let him be adopted by Mrs. Jones.

After Mrs. Jones had left, Bianca had informed Jeremiah that she was going to confess their lie to Mrs. Jones before she left for her retreat. Jeremiah had laughed as he suggested that perhaps they might need to wait until she returned when she was destined to be in a more forgiving state. He had also shared that he thought they should talk to Mrs. Jones together, but Bianca felt that since she was the reason they were in the current situation, it was her responsibility to handle the matter. Jeremiah had accepted Bianca's logic, but he knew that when the time was right, he'd apologize to Mrs. Jones in his own way. Although she obviously already accepted him as a member of her extended family, he needed her to accept him as more because clearly he planned to make Bianca a part of his family. To accomplish that with Mrs. Jones's blessings, he needed her to see him as worthy of Bianca.

*****

While they watched a movie after dinner, Jeremiah thought to himself that he was glad he'd seen the movie he'd selected at least ten times because Bianca was much more enjoyable to watch than any movie he'd ever seen. He was also glad that Mrs. Jones had declined their offer to join them for their movie night. He would not have wanted Mrs. Jones to witness the fact that he had eyes only for Bianca and not the science fiction thriller he'd selected.

Bianca had started off sitting on the far end of the sofa with the popcorn bowl between them. But each time she'd become frightened by the alien monsters, she'd moved closer and closer to Jeremiah, at one point placing the bowl on the cocktail table in front of them. Now she was practically sitting in his lap she was huddled so closely to him. Feeling that he might've gone overboard with his choice, he'd offered to switch to a calmer movie shortly after they'd begun watching the movie, but Bianca had insisted that she was fine. Of course, Jeremiah had expected she'd respond in that manner after he'd teased her about not being able to hang with the "big dogs." Bianca was not one to back down from a dare or threat of any kind. That was one of the traits he admired in her. Unfortunately for Bianca though, Jeremiah's appreciation of the character trait didn't stop him from using it to badger her. As Bianca leaned in to Jeremiah, the apple fragrance of her shampoo permeated his senses. How such an innocent scent could be so arousing escaped Jeremiah.

As Jeremiah watched Bianca, he wondered again what had happened to take her away from him. There'd been a time when he'd been free to just pull her into his arms at any time, no questions asked. And then poof! All of that was gone. Dammit! He wanted what they'd had in the past back again.

Allowing the mischievous male gene inside of him to take over and guide his actions, Jeremiah timed his next move perfectly. At the same moment the alien monster reached out to claim its prey with a snarling growl, Jeremiah grasped Bianca's upper arms emitting a loud "Gotcha!"

Bianca screamed and plunged into his arms before pulling away in the next instant. "Jeremiah! Why'd you do that?"

"I couldn't help it. You looked like you were just waiting, and I couldn't resist," he responded laughing wholeheartedly as he pulled Bianca back close to him and placed his hand on her cheek.

"Jeremiah, I'm going to kick your butt," Bianca announced struggling to ignore the feel of his touch on her face as she gazed into his eyes, immediately stripping Jeremiah of all self control.

"I apologize," he stated bringing his other hand to her face and drowning in the sea of chocolate promises.

"You should apologize. You scared me," Bianca remarked trying to remain unmoved by the intimacy of their position.

"Oh, I'm not apologizing for that. You should know I will do that again. You make it too easy not to. I'm apologizing for this." With that, Jeremiah closed the remaining distance between them bringing his lips to hers, barely touching at first and then claiming her lips as only he could.

Now it was Bianca's turn to drown. She'd thought she remembered the precision with which Jeremiah had kissed her. It was not as if she'd kissed many men before him, but a few had kissed her after that summer. None had completed the task with the finesse of Jeremiah. On those rare occasions, when she'd been kissed by others, Bianca had attributed her evaluations of the other parties' shortcomings to her unfair comparisons to exaggerated memories of Jeremiah's skills.

Now Bianca realized her memories paled in light of the real thing. Why had she left all those years ago? What had she been afraid of? That one kiss hinted at so many promises worth pursuing, Bianca couldn't believe she'd taken herself away from what had been offered.

One second Bianca was questioning all that had occurred between the two of them, particularly the part where she'd run home to a bland, safe life of school and family. The next, she felt abandoned as Jeremiah removed his lips from hers, pulling himself away.

Stunned, Bianca looked at Jeremiah poised to question him. Before her state of mind would allow her mouth to form a question,

Jeremiah's words penetrated her fog.

"Good night, Bianca. I'll see you in the morning," he responded, clearly dismissing her.

"But...?"

"No, buts. You go on and go to bed. I'll be fine."

~~~~~

CHAPTER NINE

Jeremiah was nowhere near fine, and he was definitely not going to the place with the pearly gates after the lie he'd just told Bianca. What in the world had he just done?

It had not been his intention to kiss Bianca senseless. No more than he'd planned to drown himself in her pure essence. One minute he'd been planning the perfect time to scare Bianca, and the next he couldn't help himself. She was so close, and her succulent lips offered up promises he simply couldn't resist. Jeremiah had a clear mental plan for reclaiming Bianca, and what had just happened was not on that list. He wouldn't be surprised if Bianca caught the next flight back to Chicago. Away from him once again. Away from their future. He had better get himself under control before everything was lost. All he knew was that if he had not sent Bianca to bed when he had, he'd not have been able to refrain from making mad, passionate love to her right there on the family room sofa. And that is certainly not how he wanted their first time to be.

After a night of tossing and turning, Jeremiah finally willed himself to fall asleep in the wee hours of the morning. He still didn't have a plan for his next step, but he trusted that when he woke up, he'd be thinking more clearly. After at least a couple hours of sleep and a hot cup of coffee, he'd be ready to face Bianca and anything she might say. The last thing he wanted was to have frightened Bianca, but he knew he wouldn't know how she'd responded until he saw her in the morning. Once he saw her, he'd have a better idea of how to proceed.

*****

Jeremiah might have been fine, Bianca thought. But she was anything but. That one kiss had raised all sorts of questions in her mind, the first of which was 'So what now?' Obviously, Jeremiah still had strong feelings for her. It was no longer just a matter of her keeping her own feelings to herself. They had to figure out what to do with the emotions she'd thought they both had put to rest. Emotions that seemingly had lay dormant waiting for the right moment to present themselves again. Bianca had already acknowledged to herself that she was obviously still in love with Jeremiah. Now they had to deal with his feelings. When they had had "the talk," Jeremiah had made it clear that he'd been hurt when she'd left ten years ago. Was it possible that he still had feelings for her? Was it possible that they could pick up where they'd left off? What if she didn't like the man he'd become? That was doubtful, but Bianca accepted that it could happen. Or worse, yet, what if Jeremiah didn't like the woman she'd become? What if what she thought he might be feeling now was really the result of his having to depend on her for his care. Hadn't she read once about patients developing strong feelings for their nurses? Something about a Florence Nightingale complex or syndrome or something.

For the second night in a row, Bianca had not slept well. Yesterday, she'd wakened exhausted from the crazy nightmares she'd had about showering with Jeremiah. This morning, she'd wakened alert and wired like a child on Christmas morning anticipating the wonder and uncontainable excitement of the day. Her nerves tingled from pure energy that emanated from the raw emotions seeking release.

At least an hour earlier than normal, she donned her exercise attire and after checking on Jeremiah to ensure he was still sleeping, she stepped into the pre-dawn morning to begin her morning walk. Today, she expected she'd actually run more than walk, determined to use physical exertion to clear her mind. As she alternated between walking and running, she let her mind wander. There was no doubt in her mind that she and Jeremiah needed to talk about what had happened last night. Jeremiah had essentially sent her to bed the night before like a chastised child, deliberately halting any conversation on the topic. But they could not avoid the matter indefinitely.

What if Jeremiah regretted kissing her? Of course, in the midst, it hadn't seemed as if he regretted his actions. When he'd kissed her ten years ago, Bianca had been innocent and naïve. Unaware of where one kiss could ultimately lead. Last night with just a little urging, Bianca would've ended up in Jeremiah's bed only to later regret having lost control in the home of two of her best friends.

Throughout her exercise routine, Bianca probed possible outcomes of the kiss. Part of her mind welcomed the idea that she and Jeremiah might move forward or continue where they'd left off ten years ago. The other part convinced her that what had happened the night before was an anomaly--an event that had occurred with no reason and no possibility of repeating itself. The only thing she continued to be sure of was that she and Jeremiah had to talk about what had happened.

The phone was ringing when Bianca entered the house after her combination walk-run no more calm than when she'd begun. She suspected that Jeremiah was still sleeping as had been the case when she'd left the house, but she didn't worry about the phone waking him as she'd turned down the volume on all the ringers on the phones to keep the phones from waking Jeremiah. Not recognizing the number on the caller ID, she let the answering machine pick up the call as had become her practice since taking up temporary residence at Marissa and Steve's.

"Jeremiah, this is your mom," were the first words of the message.

Hearing that the caller was Jeremiah's mother, Bianca almost picked up the receiver, but she didn't want to be the one to tell Jeremiah's mom that he'd been injured or that it was all her fault. She decided she'd just let Jeremiah call his mom when he woke up. Surely he knew how to deal with his mom in situations like this. She knew how her parents and sisters would respond if they found out she'd been sick or hurt for days and hadn't contacted them.

"I have not heard from you in almost a week," his mom continued. "I am starting to worry about you. I've left several voice mail messages on your cell phone. I know you're on vacation, but if you don't call me by the end of today, I am calling the police."

Once Jeremiah's mom ended her message, Bianca peeked into the guest suite and finding Jeremiah still asleep, continued her morning routine with her shower. When she was dressed, she went to check on Jeremiah again and found him wide awake and fully dressed. It might've been her imagination, but Jeremiah seemed a bit flustered, definitely not his normal calm, teasing self. Perhaps that kiss had rattled him as much as it had affected her. "How are you feeling?" She asked, automatically straightening the covers on his bed as she worked hard to mask her nervousness. "Are you ready for breakfast? I've got a breakfast casserole ready to go into the oven. Your mom called while you were asleep. She seemed pretty upset. You better call her before she calls the police." Even to her own ears, the last part sounded rushed.

"What?" Jeremiah responded realizing that he'd been so focused on watching Bianca looking for signs that would indicate her mood that he'd not really been listening to what she said.

"I was saying, your mom called," Bianca repeated, slowly this time, actually stopping to look at Jeremiah directly. "She said something about leaving messages on your cell phone and you not calling her back. I can't believe you haven't called your family. Your mom is really worried about you."

Jeremiah groaned loudly before saying, "I was going to call them when I felt a little better. Knowing my mom, she'll come to check on me with an entourage. I was hoping to put that off as long as possible."

"Close family, huh? Jeremiah, you never told me you were a mama's boy," Bianca, responded laughing, feeling the release of at least a little of the tension she'd been holding in.

"If by 'mama's boy' you mean spoiled brat who always gets his way, you are way off. My mom doesn't play that. She's just really protective of her 'babies.' You'd better be sure you're ready for this," Jeremiah responded reaching for his cell phone.

"I'll be in the kitchen," Bianca announced shaking her head as she left the room to give Jeremiah privacy while he spoke with his mom.

*****

One thing Jeremiah had learned from his mother was that the best offense was a pleading defense. When his mom answered her phone on the second ring, he launched into his humble apology. Just as he'd predicted, as soon as his mom learned that he'd re-injured his knee, she informed him that she and his dad were coming to check on him. From what she'd shared, she'd been planning to come to Houston with his dad on a business trip regarding opening a new office anyway. That was why she'd been so anxious to connect with Jeremiah. She knew he was on vacation, but she had no idea whether or not he'd be in town. When he'd missed his weekly call to her, she'd begun to worry.

As he hung up the phone, Jeremiah acknowledged yet another twist in his master plan. With his parents' impending arrival in two days, he no longer had the luxury of postponing his inevitable conversation with Bianca. The last thing he needed was for his mom to know he was in love with Bianca before Bianca knew. And he knew his mom had only to look at him in the presence of Bianca to know the truth. His problem now was how to broach the subject with Bianca. It was too bad his parents were coming to Houston so soon. Jeremiah would have preferred going home for a few days to visit them leaving Bianca safely in Houston away from questioning and gossiping family members. He and Bianca definitely needed to figure out what they were going to do with their relationship before his family arrived.

*****

While Jeremiah talked with his mom and pondered his next move, Bianca preheated the oven and enjoyed a cup of coffee, as she speculated on what kind of people Jeremiah's family would be. She suspected that they'd be down to earth like Jeremiah. Although the family was quite wealthy now, she knew his parents and a couple uncles had started their extremely lucrative trucking company when Jeremiah had been a baby. Bianca could not recall all of the details, but when she and Jeremiah had dated years ago, he'd spoken a lot about his family. Apparently, they were really close and looked out for one another as family should. Not that her family didn't look out for one another, but she remembered that when Jeremiah had talked about his family, she'd felt a bit envious.

The stories Jeremiah had shared about the antics of him and his siblings had kept her laughing. Even though she had two sisters, the fact that they were five years older and twins had kept Bianca from developing a tight relationship with them. For one thing, they'd always viewed her as the baby and never as an equal. And the second thing is that she'd never felt she could penetrate that twin bubble for which twins were famous. Jeremiah had twin sisters, too, so he totally got what Bianca had meant when she'd shared information about how she'd always felt like an outsider in her own home. From what Bianca remembered, Jeremiah and his two brothers had pretty much just looked after the girls because they were the babies and the only girls. Bianca expected she'd get along fine with Jeremiah's family. Her problem revolved around how she and Jeremiah were going to deal with their current situation. Whatever that situation was.

When Jeremiah joined Bianca in the kitchen a few minutes later shortly after she put the casserole in the oven, the look on his face told her he really was not happy with the outcome of his conversation with his mom.

"My parents are coming on Thursday."

"Jeremiah, that look on your face does not match the message that your parents are coming. Is everything okay?" Bianca felt her heart tighten in anticipation of what Jeremiah might say.

"We need to talk." Jeremiah blurted as he took a seat at the head of the table to Bianca's left. Taking her hands in his, Jeremiah looked directly into her eyes. "Last night..." he began and then continued after a brief pause. "I didn't mean to kiss you..."

"I know, you apologized," Bianca responded pulling her hands away from his as she mentally prepared herself for rejection.

"No, you can't know what I mean," he grasped her hands again, this time more tightly. He felt more than saw her shoulders go rigid. It amazed him that he could still read Bianca so well even after all these years. "I know I apologized..." he continued again after a short pause. "But I wasn't apologizing for kissing you...per se...This is not coming out right." Jeremiah paused again, trying to figure out how to proceed.

"Jeremiah, just say it. You are making me nervous," Bianca responded trying desperately to reclaim her hands again. "I can take whatever you have to say." It was a lie, but Jeremiah didn't need to know that. She might not be able to readily handle whatever he had to say, but she was determined to accept whatever he said like the grown woman she was.

"That's the problem," he responded holding her hands even more tightly. "I don't mean to make you nervous. And I didn't mean to make you nervous last night." The tears glistening in her eyes forced him to get to his point. "The thing of it is, Bianca..." Bringing her hands to his lips, he kissed them before continuing, never taking his eyes from hers. "I love you...I've always loved you. I will probably always love you....When you left before, I was devastated...Afterward, I threw myself into my studies trying to forget you and everything we'd had. And I thought I had, but...when I saw you last week, everything came back to me. I realized I'd never stopped loving you. That's why I was so upset that night at Mrs. Jones's. Then when you said you'd really cared about me back then, I knew I wanted to try again. I just wanted to give you time before…"

"Oh, Jeremiah," Bianca interrupted unable to hold back any longer. "I love you, too. You don't know the thoughts that have been going through my head since last night. When you apologized and then kissed me and sent me to bed, I thought you might be fighting a Florence Nightingale complex or whatever it's called."

"What? Come here, girl," Jeremiah released Bianca's hands just long enough to slide her chair towards his. Then he reclaimed her hands pulling Bianca as close as the chairs and table leg would allow. "I just want us to start all over again or to pick up where we left off. I don't know all the details. I just know I want you in my life, and I don't want to lose you again. And I don't want to do anything to push you away. Last night, I thought I might have done just that."

Jeremiah's unbridled honesty was Bianca's undoing. She felt the protective shell around her heart break open. The words that followed spilled forth of their own volition. "Oh Jeremiah… All those years ago, I didn't leave because of anything you did. Oh, I hate that you thought that. Oh, I was so in love with you. I'd never experienced that before, and it was overwhelming. I loved the way I felt when I was around you and the way I felt when I thought about you when we weren't together. I was in Heaven. And then my mom called one day and told me she and my dad were getting a divorce. I was crushed. You can't know how hearing that one word shattered my world. My parents loved one another. I'm sure of it. And they were getting a divorce after 25 years of marriage. All my life men had rejected me. In high school and then before I met you in college. For some reason they always found me lacking. I wasn't beautiful or sexy enough. I'd felt so ashamed for so long. My sisters never had that problem with men. And then I met you, and my world turned upside down. Everything with you, with us, was perfect. You made me feel beautiful and wanted…And then when my mom called, all I could think was that eventually I'd lose you too. That you'd find me lacking and dump me like everyone else. I couldn't let that happen again. So I bailed before you could bail on me. I am so sorry you thought any of that had anything to do with you…"

She'd had him at "I love you, too," but Jeremiah listened to all Bianca had to say up to the part about her being sorry. Then, he couldn't hold himself away from her any longer. They'd hash out the details later, especially the part about her being lacking, but now Bianca was his again. Now he wanted her in his arms where she belonged. Had it not been for his injured knee, he'd have pulled her into his lap, but for now, he settled for drawing Bianca as close as physically possible, wrapping his arms around her, and sealing their love with a kiss that welcomed them both back where they belonged.

~~~~~

CHAPTER TEN

From Tuesday morning until Thursday afternoon Bianca had been so busy preparing for Jeremiah's parents' visit she'd not had time to devote to thinking about the new status of her relationship with Jeremiah. She was a bit nervous about meeting Jeremiah's family, but she was in a state of emotional turmoil about the decision she and Jeremiah had made to renew their relationship. A part of her was ecstatic. She wanted to be with Jeremiah as part of a couple again, but her old self-doubts kept rearing through her positive spirits. Obviously, they both still had strong feelings for one another. But what if she and Jeremiah pursued their relationship and he found her unworthy as others had in the past? She couldn't imagine that she'd find him unworthy. The part of her that worried about their relationship surviving felt that it was probably best to just leave their relationship alone—as just two people who used to date. She also worried that she and Jeremiah would lose the level of friendship they currently experienced.

Of course that kiss they'd shared on Tuesday morning had had nothing to do with friendship. Bianca still shuddered when she allowed herself to recall the moment Jeremiah had pulled her into his arms. If relationships could survive on chemistry alone, she and Jeremiah would have no problems. Too bad that wasn't how things worked.

One good thing in her opinion was that they'd agreed to take it slowly, in fact, to almost start over again. Jeremiah wanted to take her on a date. Said he didn't want her to miss out on the romance she deserved. He'd also said he didn't want Bianca to have any unfounded ideas that he was attracted to her because of some complex or syndrome she'd read about. So they'd agreed that they'd put off having an actual relationship until Jeremiah's doctor released him and he could start courting her with their new "first date."

After they'd kissed Tuesday morning, she and Jeremiah had been spending their time catching each other up on what had happened over the past ten years, purposely limiting their physical contact to light touches and chaste kisses. She had to admit that similar to their previous relationship, it seemed that they could barely be in close proximity to one another without one of them reaching out to touch the other, even if only on the arm, back, or shoulder. Bianca wasn't sure about Jeremiah, but for her, the constant touching only heightened her emotional and physical response to Jeremiah. Their first official date could not come soon enough for the part of her that relished their upcoming relationship. That date was hanging over her head like an albatross for the part of her that was driven by self-doubts.

Bianca also acknowledged that while she and Jeremiah had shared information about their respective pasts, neither of them had revealed details related to their previous engagements. She knew what had happened in her own situation. But what about Jeremiah's? Bianca had learned from Marissa that Jeremiah had gotten engaged and then later that he was no longer engaged. But neither had she asked nor Marissa shared any particular details. It made sense to Bianca that neither she nor Jeremiah could move forward without addressing why they both had been engaged, but neither of them had gotten married.

On Tuesday morning after she and Jeremiah had talked about renewing their relationship and had finally eaten breakfast, Bianca had cleaned up the kitchen and then walked over to Mrs. Jones's house to confess her transgressions regarding having kept her relationship with Jeremiah a secret ten years ago as well as purposely letting Mrs. Jones think they'd just met during Bianca's current visit. Jeremiah had told Bianca that he'd informed his mom that he and Bianca had met years ago, but he hadn't gone into specifics regarding the details he'd given his mom about their previous relationship. Since Jeremiah's mom knew they'd met before, Bianca was determined to clear the air with Mrs. Jones before Jeremiah's family arrived in town. The last thing she wanted was for Mrs. Davis to say something in front of Mrs. Jones about Jeremiah knowing Bianca from years ago. If that happened, Bianca feared that Mrs. Jones would be hurt, and it could ruin her relationship with Mrs. Jones.

Not surprisingly, Mrs. Jones had accepted Bianca's apology graciously, laughing as she'd shared with Bianca that she totally understood why Bianca and Marissa had kept Bianca's relationship with Jeremiah a secret during that long ago summer. Mrs. Jones had even shared with Bianca that Jeremiah must really care for her if he'd been willing to not give her secret away that night at the dinner table. When Mrs. Jones had made the statement about Jeremiah's feelings, Bianca had shared bits and pieces from the conversations they'd had the night of the dinner as well as from Tuesday morning. Mrs. Jones was pleased that Bianca and Jeremiah had made the decision to give their relationship another chance. She'd even shared that she thought the two of them made a great couple. Mrs. Jones had admitted that she didn't know Jeremiah very well, but over the years of coming in contact with him and his family at various events, she'd come to know him well enough to see that he was a kind person with a good heart.

What had surprised Bianca was that Mrs. Jones had instructed her to evaluate what had caused her and Jeremiah to end their relationship years ago and to be sure that any unresolved issues had been addressed before they moved forward. Mrs. Jones had even suggested that perhaps Bianca might want to discuss her fears about relationships and marriage with her mom. Mrs. Jones had told Bianca that as a mother she'd want to know if her daughter were troubled about anything. Mrs. Jones had also said that while Bianca's mom might not go into any particular details about her parents' divorce, Mrs. Jones thought Bianca's mom might be able to help Bianca to separate their experiences from her own. Bianca had promised Mrs. Jones that she would definitely speak with her mom about the situation. As she'd spoken with Mrs. Jones, Bianca had realized that she'd never spoken with her sisters or her parents about any of the details related to their divorce or about how the divorce had affected her. Bianca's sisters had both been in graduate school at the time and were completing internships in Europe when Bianca had gotten the call from her mother. By the time her sisters had returned home, their dad had moved out of the house. Shortly after their return, Bianca's sisters had moved out of the house beginning their own careers and leaving just Bianca and her mom in the family home. With Bianca away at school most of the time, they only saw one another around holidays.

During Bianca's visit with Mrs. Jones, they'd planned the meal menus for the long weekend with Jeremiah's parents, gone grocery shopping, and chopped vegetables and pecans for various dishes before Bianca had returned to her temporary home and immediately begun a cleaning spree fit for a white glove inspection.

*****

Thursday afternoon Jeremiah watched Bianca as she flitted around wiping at nonexistent spots and invisible dust mites. It hadn't occurred to him before now, but her actions indicated that she was obviously nervous about meeting his family. He couldn't imagine why she'd be nervous; he knew everyone would love her. She had that effect on people.

When he'd initially spoken with his mom about his injury, he'd tried to convince her that he was okay because he was not alone. He'd explained that Bianca, a friend of Steve and Marissa's who was visiting, was helping him during his convalescence period. Of course, he'd had to explain how Bianca had come to be visiting while Steve and Marissa were in Europe. He'd also told his mom that he'd met Bianca years ago so she was not a stranger. He'd added the latter because his mom had been outraged that his medical care was in the hands of a complete stranger. Although he'd made sure his mom knew, Bianca was not a stranger, Jeremiah had purposely left out details related to the status of his relationship with Bianca because he'd been unsure of how to describe their situation. He didn't expect that his mother would've been satisfied with "It's complicated."

After he and Bianca had talked and agreed to give their relationship a second chance, Jeremiah had considered calling his mom back, but then he'd decided it was probably best to just wait. If things went according to his plans, his family would know what they needed to know soon enough. And the last thing he wanted to do was to put Bianca in an uncomfortable position with his family. If he announced their relationship, and things didn't work out, he didn't want anyone blaming her. Hoping to tease Bianca into relaxing, he called out, "Come on, Bianca. You're just avoiding me because you know I'm getting ready to take back some of my countries you stole from me."

"I'll be there in a minute." She replied as she continued dusting furniture. "I just want to make sure everything is right. I don't want your mom thinking you're convalescing in a pig sty. And I did not steal your countries from you. I won them fair and square. You're just being a sorry loser."

"My mom taught me how to clean, so if the house is dirty, she's going to blame me and not you. If it's dirty, she'll know that it had to be dirty before I got hurt."

When Bianca joined Jeremiah a few minutes later to continue their Risk game, she laughed as she asked, "Okay, Mr. Jeremiah, what makes you think today is going to be any different from yesterday and the days before? You must be planning to cheat today." After studying the board, she removed the Post-it note she'd stuck on the table the night before to remind them where they'd left off. "Okay, it's your turn."

They were in the midst of their game when Jeremiah's family arrived.

*****

When Jeremiah had warned Bianca that his mom would come to visit with an entourage, Bianca had thought he'd been exaggerating. But when she'd opened the door late that afternoon and Mrs. Davis had entered with Mr. Davis, Jeremiah's eldest brother, Aaron, and Paris, one of his twin sisters, Bianca had almost found herself looking for the family dog.

Throughout their visit, Jeremiah's parents and brother had been enlightening Bianca and Mrs. Jones with tales of Jeremiah's wild and checkered childhood while they all simultaneously played one board game after another. Paris added to the entertainment by including details regarding all of her brothers' efforts to protect her and her twin sister, Alexandria, from the woes of teenage boys.

Although Jeremiah had winced from time to time and told his side of individual stories, Bianca thought he took the friendly ribbing in great spirits. However, she soon learned he had an entirely different response to the games they played. Paris was the Queen of Clue and Sorry. Bianca held the reins in Risk, but she suspected that was because the game was new to Jeremiah and his family. Jeremiah, apparently, was truly the King of Monopoly with his family although he'd yet to beat Bianca when they'd played with one another. Bianca thought that perhaps that would soon change as Jeremiah had obviously notched his competitive spirit up a bit for the family. The words cut throat came to her mind.

Bianca was actually getting a kick out of watching Jeremiah interact with his family. The pecking order emulated the children's birth order. Jeremiah being the middle boy, on some issues, deferred to his brother who was older than him by two years, but obviously gave Paris, five years his junior, no leeway. All of the siblings clearly respected their parents, but the games were neutral territories with no mercy shown for anyone.

Observing Jeremiah with his family had also given Bianca the opportunity to identify where Jeremiah had gotten his looks and demeanor. He'd clearly inherited his dad's rugged good looks and muscular build, but he definitely had his mother's skin tone, hazel eyes with gold specks, and her warm, welcoming smile. All three of the children Bianca had met had inherited specific aspects of their parents' traits and mannerisms. The twins, who Bianca knew were identical, were obviously the image of a younger version of their mom. Bianca suspected that Matthew, the youngest son also resembled his parents.

*****

Jeremiah's family and Mrs. Jones had left close to midnight on Thursday night only to return early Friday morning for breakfast. Bianca had prepared another of her specialty breakfast casseroles for the occasion. After breakfast Jeremiah's dad, brother and sister had all left for the expansion meeting for the family trucking business. When everyone else had left, Bianca had excused herself to allow Mrs. Davis to spend time with Jeremiah while she worked on her manuscript. Bianca's self-imposed deadline for completing her first draft was fast approaching, and she was behind on her own schedule. She was pleased to know that she'd accomplished quite a bit that afternoon before Jeremiah's dad, brother and sister had returned from their business meeting.

After a lunch of leftover pizza and salad from the night before, following Jeremiah's directions, Aaron had driven everyone out to the site of Jeremiah's new home. When they'd arrived, Mrs. Davis had forbidden Jeremiah from walking on the rough ground surface with his crutches, forcing him to wait in the car while his family took themselves on a tour. Bianca had waited in the car with Jeremiah. Bianca thought Jeremiah had looked especially pleased when she'd informed him that she wanted the pleasure of seeing his house for the first time with him. While Jeremiah's family had toured his new home, it had taken all of Bianca's energy to keep Jeremiah from kissing her into a frenzy and steaming up the car windows during his family's absence.

*****

As Bianca washed the dinner dishes with Mrs. Davis Friday night, she acknowledged that she'd worried unnecessarily about meeting Jeremiah's family. She'd liked everyone immediately. And from what she could tell, they'd responded to her in a similar fashion. At first, it had seemed to Bianca that his mom was taking in everything trying to assess how well Jeremiah was being cared for. His dad and his siblings seemed to just take everything in stride waiting for some sort of magic signal from their mom that the coast was clear. She and Jeremiah had not actually discussed how they'd present their relationship to his family so Bianca had figured she'd just follow Jeremiah's lead. From what Bianca could tell, his family accepted her as just one of Marissa and Steve's never ending house guests who just happened to be looking after Jeremiah during his healing period.

"Jeremiah tells me you all knew each other years ago." Mrs. Davis's comment interrupted Bianca thoughts.

"Yes, Ma'am, we actually met the first summer I came to visit Marissa," she responded hoping Jeremiah's mother didn't think she and Jeremiah knew each other in the Biblical sense. "Marissa and I met our freshman year in college, and I came home with her during Spring Break our freshman and sophomore years. After our sophomore year, I came for an internship at Reverend Jones's church. That's when I met Jeremiah." Even to her own ears, Bianca sounded like she was rambling. She hated that nervous habit of hers.

"Bianca, I appreciate that your parents raised you well, but I only allow family under twenty-one to address me as 'Ma'am,' and you, my dear, are family. Turning to face Bianca, Mrs. Davis continued. "You can call me Mrs. Davis, Fiona, or FiFi, but not Ma'am." After a brief pause, she added, "I want you to know I truly appreciate your looking after Jeremiah. I was worried before I got here. But now I know he's in capable hands."

"Thank you, Mrs. Davis, FiFi…" Bianca responded, purposely choosing the least formal name for Jeremiah's mom. "Well, I would've helped Jeremiah anyway, but he fell trying to keep me from falling, so I feel especially obligated to helping him to heal." The day before Bianca had caught what must've been the tail end of Jeremiah's explanation of how he'd re-injured his knee. She'd heard FiFi remind Jeremiah that he was not as young as he'd been when he'd initially torn his ACL and she'd told him that if he didn't follow his doctor's orders, he could suffer a relapse.

When FiFi stated that Jeremiah had not provided the family with all of the particulars related to his re-injury, Bianca had shared the details of their collaborative rescue of Little Trouble.

"Listen, Bianca," FiFi continued when Bianca had completed her story. "Jeremiah told me that you're working on a book based on your dissertation. He also told me that you've been so busy looking after him, that you haven't been able to get much work done on your manuscript. So I've got a plan that will give you time to work without interruptions for most of the day tomorrow. It will also give me a chance to visit with Jeremiah for a spell."

At first Bianca, wanted to protest FiFi's plans for allowing Bianca to work all day in Paris's hotel room on Saturday, but she realized that doing so might offend Jeremiah's mom. FiFi certainly had a right to spend time with her own son. And Bianca did need the time to work. She was pleased with what she'd been able to complete during the few hours she'd devoted to the manuscript that day. If she spent the better part of the day working tomorrow, she could tackle so much more. Plus, she might even take the opportunity to call her mom while she could talk to her privately about what was on her mind.

*****

Later that night, after his family left, Jeremiah watched Bianca as she wiped down the appliances and the counters in the kitchen. Throughout the evening, he'd felt more than seen his mom's piercing eyes on him, but each time he'd looked in her direction, she'd been looking at something or someone other than him. With his peripheral vision, he'd also caught incidents of his mom signaling something to his dad, but again, when he'd look directly at either of his parents, they appeared to be focused on the game they were playing. As he'd expected, his family had responded well to Bianca, welcoming her as if they'd known her as long as he had. They'd never opened up to Samantha that way. It might've been because they hadn't met Samantha until he and Samantha were seeing each other seriously, but Jeremiah thought it had more to do with Samantha's personality. Bianca was a warm, caring individual who naturally invited others to reciprocate that kindness. Samantha was none of those things. His mom had even invited Bianca to call her by her nickname. She'd never offered that opportunity to Samantha.

Even from the family room, Jeremiah could tell that Bianca was nervous about something so he grabbed his crutches and joined her in the kitchen area. "Are you going to be okay?" He asked, taking the dish cloth from her hand and turning Bianca to face him. "My mom told me about her plan for tomorrow. I hope you're okay with it. You can try to back out of it if you want, but if you haven't already figured it out, my mom can be kind of stubborn when she sets her mind to something."

"I'll be fine," Bianca responded. "Yes, I did pick up on where you got your stubborn streak," she added chuckling. "I just don't want to impose on Paris's space." It felt good to stand this close to Jeremiah. Bianca had purposely been keeping her physical distance from Jeremiah in the presence of his family. She realized that she'd missed his touch.

"Trust me when I say, Paris would not let you in her space, if she didn't want you there. Look at it this way. You'll be able to get some work done without waiting on me. And I won't be tempted to do this." With that Jeremiah cupped Bianca's chin with his free hand and closed the short distance between them by bringing his lips to hers.

Bianca allowed herself to be drawn into the kiss. Each time Jeremiah kissed her, she was reminded of what she'd left behind all those years ago. She also acknowledged how much both of them had changed during the absence. When she'd been nineteen, she'd had no inkling of all of the parts of her body that could respond to a kiss. Now, each time Jeremiah kissed her, it was as if she drowned in his essence. The more they reacquainted themselves with one another, the more she gave of herself, simultaneously trusting Jeremiah more and more. When Jeremiah pulled away, Bianca found herself speechless for a moment and catching her breath.

"Yeah, well…we definitely want to limit any temptations you may have to do that." She responded when she'd regained a semblance of composure. "Now let me finish in here. You need to go somewhere and elevate your leg."

"That is true," Jeremiah answered, retrieving the crutch he'd lain to the side and heading toward the guest suite. "I probably need to ice my knee again before I go to bed. I can be feeling just fine when I'm sitting down, but then when I stand up, it seems like my knee is going to explode."

"You're just ending your first week of healing," Bianca chuckled. "The nurse said the second week you shouldn't be in as much pain if you continue to keep the weight off, elevate your leg and ice it throughout the day. Go on and get yourself situated, and I'll bring you an ice pack before I turn in."

~~~~~

CHAPTER ELEVEN

The next morning, Bianca rose early in preparation for her day away from the house. Although she dressed in workout gear, she postponed her exercise routine knowing that she'd take brisk walks throughout the day to help her to think about her writing. Because FiFi's plan for the day included bringing breakfast from the hotel restaurant, Bianca only made coffee and set the dining room table before returning to the den to pack her bags.

She wasn't sure how much she needed to pack, but she expected she'd be gone anywhere from six to eight hours which would seem like an eternity if she left something she needed behind. She knew it would be better to have something she didn't need rather than for her to be missing something she needed. With that thought, she packed up what she'd considered her traveling office when she'd packed for her sabbatical. Her printer, manuscripts, and laptop all fit in the padded overnight bag with the in-line skate wheels. Her insulated lunch bag held snacks, coffee, tea, and water, and she had even stuffed a few extra snacks in her purse.

When Jeremiah's family arrived with breakfast, Bianca's bags were sitting by the front door, and she and Jeremiah were drinking coffee in the family room. After breakfast, FiFi shooed Bianca out of the kitchen telling her that she'd clean up while Paris drove Bianca to the hotel. Next, FiFi instructed Aaron to load Bianca's bags into the car.

After Bianca gave FiFi details regarding Jeremiah's medicine and ice schedule, she and Paris left the house.

"Thanks for letting me camp out in your room for the day. I hope it's not a problem," Bianca stated realizing that this time in the car represented the first time she'd engaged in a conversation with Paris without at least one other member of the family present. "I appreciate the opportunity to work uninterrupted, but I know how I am about my space."

"Oh, no. It's not a problem," Paris responded. "We really appreciate everything you're doing for Jeremiah. We just want to help you out any way we can. I know Jeremiah can be a hand full when he's not one hundred percent. Doesn't like anyone catering to him, even when it's doctor's orders."

"You definitely know your brother," Bianca stated, "but surprisingly, Jeremiah's taking his two-week respite seriously. He's been relatively good about following his doctor's orders, so far, but he has another week to go. We shall see how he handles being cooped up in the house for another week."

"Better you than me," Paris added with a laugh.

When they arrived at Paris's room, Paris invited Bianca to use the micro-fridge and coffee pot during the day. She even told Bianca to feel free to take a nap on one of the double beds if she found herself sleepy. She also shared that the hotel had a fitness center. Bianca chuckled and thanked Paris for the offer, telling Paris that while she would exercise by taking short walks every couple of hours, she had no intention of using the fitness center or taking a nap.

Once Paris left, Bianca set up her temporary office on the desk, wrote out a schedule for the day, and got to work. She wasn't sure exactly how much she could accomplish, but she planned to work a good two hours before she took a break. She'd even written into her schedule a time to call her mom. It never ceased to amaze Bianca that a significant portion of what she'd been required to include in her dissertation needed to be removed from the book she was writing about the same research.

She'd just completed two hours of writing when her cell phone rang. Noting that the call was from one of her sisters, she saved her work and answered the call. "Hey, Celeste. How are you? Is everything okay?" She asked starting to get a little worried. "You never call in the middle of the day, even on weekends."

"I have Serena on the other line," her sister stated causing Bianca's anxiety level to rise even more.

"Hi, Serena. I just spoke with the two of you the other day. What's up?"

"You're going to be an aunt?" The twins announced in unison.

"Wow! Congratulations! When?"

"June…" Celeste replied.

"…and July" Serena added.

"What? You both are expecting? How great is that! Either of you having twins?

"Heck no!" Serena asserted vehemently.

"Bite your tongue!" Celeste chastised before continuing, "Actually, it's too soon to tell. But I want to start with one if it's okay with the Universe."

"How are Mark and Darnell handling this news?"

"We think they're both in shock right now," Celeste explained. "But I can tell that Mark is going to be a problem. He's already hinted that I might not be able to go back to work after Christmas Break."

"But you said your baby isn't due until June."

"My point, exactly," Celeste added dryly.

After a few more minutes of chatting with her sisters, Bianca ended the call. But first, she made both of them promise to give her weekly updates on their progress. She was happy for her sisters and their husbands. She was also ecstatic about becoming an aunt twice in the upcoming year. Guiltily, she also hoped that with children of their own, neither Celeste nor Serena would continue to have the energy or time to devote to looking after their baby sister as they currently did. When Serena had inquired about how the book was coming and Bianca had shared that everything was going fine, neither had probed her for specific details. Any other time, they'd have pushed for more information such as how many words, pages or chapters she'd written. Bianca was glad they hadn't asked because she wasn't sure how she'd have been able to explain how her writing had taken a back seat to looking after Jeremiah, the prowler, who hadn't been a stranger after all.

After ending the call with her sisters, Bianca took a brisk walk, stretched her muscles, and continued working on her manuscript until the time she'd designated to call her mom. "Hi, Mommy." Bianca cheerfully greeted her mom when her mom answered her phone.

"Hi, Sweetie. How're you doing?"

"I'm doing fine. I talked to Celeste and Serena earlier. I'm excited about finally being an aunt. How do you feel about being a grandmother?"

"I think it's about time. Your dad and I have been waiting to be grandparents since Celeste got married. We thought it would never happen," her mom confided.

In the brief pause that followed her mom's confession, Bianca could almost feel when her mom tuned into her underlying mood and shifted from excited grandparent into concerned parent mode.

"Bianca, I don't think you called to talk about your sisters. What's on your mind?" Her mom asked.

"I just don't know where to begin."

"I always tell you to begin at the beginning," her mom calmly coaxed.

"Mommy, do you believe in love at first sight?"

"What kind of question is that?" Her mom responded clearly losing her calm demeanor. "Have you met someone, Bianca?"

"Well, actually I have, but I met him ten years ago."

"What? Bianca, if you met someone ten years ago why haven't we heard about him before now? And why are you asking me about this now?"

Bianca hated that she'd upset her mom. Continuing, she tried to sum up the events of that long ago summer as succinctly as possible. "Well, we met and dated that same summer you and Daddy separated. His name is Jeremiah. We met and dated and were getting kind of serious, but then when you called me and told me about you and Daddy getting a divorce, I stopped seeing him."

"Oh, Bianca. Why'd you do that?"

"I don't know, Mommy." Bianca could hear the pain in her mother's response. "I got scared…thought maybe what I was feeling wasn't real. I guess with you and Daddy breaking up…I don't know…"

"So you still haven't told me why you're bringing this up now," her mom interjected, obviously confused.

"Well, that's the thing," Bianca began. "Jeremiah is Steve's cousin, and he's here at Marissa and Steve's. I didn't know he was going to be here. And he didn't know I was coming, so things have been crazy." Quickly, Bianca gave her mother the highlights of everything that had transpired since she'd arrived, ending with details regarding how she and Jeremiah had agreed to start over again.

"So do you still have feelings for this Jeremiah?"

"Yes, Mommy, I really do. I love him. And I think he loves me, too....But..."

"Sweetie, you know I have always told you girls to follow your heart. Your heart will not steer you wrong."

"But what about what happened with you and Daddy or with me and David?"

"Sweetie, you can't hide from hurt and pain. Experiencing life to its fullest requires opening yourself up to all that life has to offer. If you love this young man, and he loves you, give each other and yourselves a chance."

For the next few minutes, Bianca relished in her mom's consoling words. She didn't even realize she was crying until she hung up the phone after they said their goodbyes. Her mom was right. She'd always told Bianca and her sisters to follow their hearts. To the contrary, Bianca had always relied on logic. Life was safer that way. Or not. She'd been logical about David, and look how that had turned out. Mrs. Jones had been right, too. Talking with her mother had been exactly what Bianca needed to help her to take the next step toward Jeremiah. While no one could guarantee that love would last forever, Bianca was willing to take a chance.

*****

Throughout the day, Jeremiah found it difficult to focus on whatever he and his family were watching, playing, or discussing. He simply couldn't help it. No matter what he and his family members were doing, his mind kept wandering to Bianca. What was she doing now? How did she feel? Did she miss him as much as he missed her? Aaron and Paris took turns teasing him about being off in space. His lack of focus was especially apparent during the Monopoly game when Paris reminded him to collect rent when Aaron landed on one of Jeremiah's properties.

Jeremiah knew his mom had planned a big farewell dinner as his family was heading back to Dallas that night, but all Jeremiah could think about was having Bianca to himself again so they could pick up where they'd left off prior to his family's visit. He and Bianca had so much to discuss, but Jeremiah knew that Bianca was still fragile. He hated that she'd never told him about her parents' divorce. He could've been a shoulder for her to lean on during that time. If he'd been there for her, she'd not have ultimately ended up with that jerk Steve had told him about. And nor would he have ended up with

Samantha.

When his mom sent Aaron and Paris to the grocery store for something she needed for dinner, Jeremiah told his dad he was going outside to get some air. He was sitting in one of the lounge chairs with his leg elevated when his mom joined him a few minutes later.

"Missing Bianca," she stated more than asked as she handed him a glass of iced tea.

"Thank you," he responded taking the glass and turning toward her. "That obvious, huh?"

"Sweetie, just so you know. I approve."

Caught totally off guard, Jeremiah barely had time to raise his eyebrows before his mom continued.

"I haven't quite figured out what's going on between you and Bianca, but I can see something is there for both of you. But Bianca is clearly staying in the den and guest bathroom and not in the guest suite with you."

Before he could open his mouth to ask his mom how she knew that, she touched her index finger to his lips and responded with that eternal response that requires no further explanation, "Don't ask. I'm a mother."

Jeremiah laughed as he hugged her and kissed his mom on the cheek. "Mom, I love you."

"I love you, too, Sweetie," she responded kissing him on his cheek before taking his hand in hers and squeezing it as she looked into his eyes. "I just want all of my children to be happy like your dad and me... Look, I accepted Samantha because you chose her. But I approve of Bianca. She's good people, and she's in love with you. And if my old eyes are not deceiving me, you're in love with her, too."

"Mom, your eyes are not old," Jeremiah countered as he hugged his mom again. "They see just as well now as they did when Aaron , Matt, and I were teenagers trying to get away with the stupid stuff teenagers try to get away with."

"Let me go," she scolded, pulling away and standing as she wiped her eyes. "If I don't get back in there now, I'll be a mess."

Jeremiah laughed to himself as his mom returned to the house. As he'd suspected, his mom had only to look at him in the presence of Bianca to know the truth of his love. If his mom also picked up on Bianca's love for him, that was an excellent sign.

When Bianca walked through the door that evening, it was all that Jeremiah could do not to go to her and welcome her back home properly. But he had no intention of calling attention to their relationship. His mom was aware something was going on between them, but he didn't want to alert the rest of his family before he and Bianca confirmed the direction in which they were headed. Jeremiah settled for calling out his greeting among those issued by his family.

Through dinner, dessert, and the final farewells, all Jeremiah could think of was holding Bianca in his arms again. As soon as Bianca closed the front door after the two of them had watched his family drive away, Jeremiah enclosed Bianca in his arms and brought his lips to hers. As he kissed her, he once again confirmed that Bianca belonged in his arms. That they belonged together.

*****

"Did you really get a lot done today, or did you just tell my mom that to keep from hurting her feelings?" Jeremiah asked later as he and Bianca sat side-by-side on the sofa. He'd draped one arm across her shoulders and absently twirled a tendril of her hair around his index finger while she turned the pages of a magazine on her lap. He was supposed to be watching the NBA exhibition game on television, but he had to keep rewinding the DVR to keep up with which team was winning. It felt good to just sit beside the woman he loved. "I hope you got a lot done," he continued, "because that's the last time you spend the day away from me until I go back to work."

"I definitely got a lot done today." Bianca responded looking up at him. "I even told my mom about you."

"Oh, yeah? What'd you tell her?" Jeremiah hadn't realized how much it mattered to him until he'd asked the question.

"I told her a little bit of everything... I told her about meeting you ten years ago and about how I'd broken things off with you after she told me about her and my dad getting divorced."

"Really?"

"Yes." Bianca continued, "And...I told her about how we talked and about how we agreed to start all over again."

Jeremiah noted that Bianca never said that she'd told her mom that she loved him. He wanted to be hurt by that, but he realized he couldn't be because he hadn't told his mom anything either. "Well my mom told me that she approved of you."

"What?" Bianca gasped. "You said something to your mom about us?" She scolded, elbowing Jeremiah in his side. Her telling her mom about him long distance on the phone was one thing. But Mrs. Davis was right here with them. What must she think?

"No, I didn't say anything to her," Jeremiah defended, rubbing his side. "Actually she said something to me. She told me she didn't know exactly what was going on, but she could see that we cared for one another. And she told me she approved of you. She also told me she could tell that we weren't living in sin because your stuff was in the den and guest bathroom and not in the guest suite." His mom hadn't actually said 'living in sin' but Jeremiah had purposely added that part to rib Bianca.

"Jeremiah! What in the world?" Bianca could feel the heat rising to her face. How had Jeremiah discussed such a thing with his mom without her knowledge? After a few seconds of silence, she asked, "Why did your mom tell you she approved of me? Are you in the habit of bringing home women your mom doesn't approve of?"

"Well, to be honest, I don't usually bring women home, but let's just say, my ex-fiancé didn't win any personality awards with my family. But let's not talk about other people. I really missed you today." Jeremiah kissed Bianca on her cheek and squeezed her to him.

"How could you miss me when you were surrounded by your family?" Bianca wondered how a kiss on the cheek could feel so endearing. "I was the one who'd been whisked away to spend the day in a hotel room all by myself."

"Believe me, I would have preferred being there with you to being here with my family." This time, Jeremiah turned Bianca's face toward his and drew her in for kiss.

Each time he kissed Bianca, Jeremiah wondered how the simple bringing together of lips and tongues could ignite such a response in him. He'd never responded to any women the way he reacted to Bianca. And it wasn't just physical. They connected on every level. It was as if they were soul mates. And he could tell that it was the same for Bianca even though he sensed that she was holding back. Obviously, those self-doubts she'd told him about were still keeping her from giving her all. Perhaps with time, she would come to know that what they had was real. He would do all he could to convince her of that. Bianca deserved romance, and he was determined to woo her. Their first date could not come soon enough for Jeremiah.

*****

As she prepared for bed that night, Bianca recalled how quickly Jeremiah had changed the subject after making that statement about his ex-fiancé not winning any personality awards with his family. What if he'd changed the subject because he still had strong feelings for his ex? Bianca knew that the ex's name was Samantha, but Marissa hadn't shared much about her, except for the fact that she, herself, hadn't cared for Samantha. Now Jeremiah had shared that his family hadn't taken to Samantha either. But what about Jeremiah? Was he still harboring feelings for her? What if he still cared for Samantha and reaching out to Bianca was his way of rebounding from the situation with Samantha?

~~~~~

CHAPTER TWELVE

When Bianca exited the den the next morning, she was shocked to see Jeremiah dressed in a dress shirt and khakis as he drank a cup of coffee. "And just where do you think you're going?" She asked.

"Good morning to you, too." Jeremiah responded. "I am going to church with you. I made coffee and heated up leftovers from yesterday's breakfast. I was just waiting for you so we could have breakfast."

"Jeremiah, you're supposed to be resting and elevating your leg, not making breakfast," Bianca scolded.

"I'm fine, Bianca. I promise I didn't put any unnecessary weight on my leg."

"What do you mean, 'unnecessary'?" Immediately, Bianca's mind conjured a picture of Jeremiah tumbling from the kitchen step stool to the floor.

"Well, I needed two hands to..."

"Jeremiah," Bianca interjected not even giving him a chance to finish his explanation. "You've already done whatever it is you did. It's probably best if I don't hear about it. Just know that if you're going to church with me, we're taking the wheelchair."

"Aww, not the wheelchair!" Jeremiah protested.

"Jeremiah, I do not want..." she began, and then changed tactics midsentence. "Okay, we're picking Mrs. Jones up so she won't have to leave her car at the church while she's away on her retreat. If you prefer, I'll let you explain to her why you're not in the wheelchair she specifically brought here for you to use."

"Now that is just playing dirty," Jeremiah complained.

"I'm just saying..." Bianca added chuckling to herself as she began serving their plates.

*****

Throughout the church service, Bianca reflected on the marvel of being reunited with Jeremiah after having been separated from him for ten years. Albeit a separation caused by her own doing. Jeremiah sat next to her in the aisle in his wheelchair. The wide aisles in the new church accommodated wheelchair seating next to the rows of cushioned chairs unlike the seating arrangement of the old church Bianca had first visited when she'd been an undergraduate. Bianca noted that a few others sat in wheelchairs in the aisles. The new arrangement was much more accommodating than having patrons in wheelchairs lined up in the back of the church.

Jeremiah had never attended church with Bianca and Marissa the summer the two of them had first met, but Bianca suspected that in the near future, they'd be attending together regularly. At least until her sabbatical ended. Although they'd declared their love for one another, they had not actually discussed the future. With Jeremiah living in Houston, and her living in Chicago, it seemed to Bianca that their future would include lots of traveling back and forth between the states. Although that idea did not especially appeal to her, she knew that she'd do whatever it took to make their relationship work. In fact, she was even willing to relocate to be with Jeremiah. It was not likely that his family's trucking company would be opening an office in Illinois, but she could probably pretty easily find a teaching job in Houston. Deciding that she would investigate the possibilities before her sabbatical ended, Bianca forced herself to focus on the reverend's message.

Sitting next to Bianca in the aisle, Jeremiah hated the attention he was drawing to himself in the wheelchair. He'd have been fine with his crutches. He'd been determined to attend church with Bianca because he wanted to show her how serious he was about her. Everyone knew that when a man attended church with a woman, he had honorable intentions. But now he questioned his decision to accompany Bianca today. Throughout the service, he'd noticed Denise and a few other women whom he'd met during the few times he'd attended the church since moving to Houston looking in his direction. He expected the wheelchair sent a message to the women that he would've preferred not to send. Jeremiah knew from previous conversations with Denise that she was recently divorced. He'd not gotten the sense that Denise was romantically interested in him. His impression was that she just appreciated having someone to talk to who didn't have ulterior motives. However, he couldn't say the same for the other women who'd introduced themselves to him. Over the past few months he'd politely circumvented invitations for coffee, lunch, dinner, drinks and more. He simply hadn't been looking to attach himself to anyone so soon after ending things with Samantha. Jeremiah smiled to himself when he thought about how quickly his intentions had changed when Bianca had come back into his life.

The curious looks from the women followed Jeremiah and Bianca after the service as she pushed him to Fellowship Hall where the hospitality committee had set up a buffet lunch of salads, sandwiches, fried chicken, and a smorgasbord of desserts. Bianca guided Jeremiah through the service line allowing him to fix his own plate before she found seats for the two of them off to the side of the room where no one would bump Jeremiah's leg. To Jeremiah, Bianca seemed oblivious to the looks they both received, but he could sense trouble brewing.

After they'd eaten, Bianca threw away their paper plates and placed their plastic cups and utensils in a recycling receptacle before informing Jeremiah that she was going to find Mrs. Jones who was meeting in one of the nearby rooms so she could tell her goodbye. No sooner had Bianca walked away from Jeremiah than Denise, Alicia, Donna and a few other women whose names Jeremiah couldn't remember swarmed him asking questions regarding what had happened to him and offering to take care of him. Jeremiah remained cordial to the women answering their questions while purposely trying not to give the impression that he was romantically interested in any one of them. It seemed to Jeremiah that Denise was tickled by his predicament. Whenever he made eye contact with her, she shrugged her shoulders and tried to hide an obvious smirk on her face. She'd warned him about some of the women at the church, but Jeremiah had assured her that he was immune to their efforts.

When Bianca returned to take Jeremiah to the car, he could tell by the tone she used to part the women who'd encircled him that she was not happy about finding him surrounded by women. Knowing what she'd experienced with her ex-fiancé, Jeremiah could only imagine what must be going through her mind. He was determined to gain and keep Bianca's trust. For without trust they'd never be able to maintain a successful relationship. He had to make it clear to her that she was the one for him. He couldn't think of a better way to start than to make a statement to his current audience. He was also determined that he and Bianca would discuss the matter later that day.

Bianca had never thought of herself as a jealous person. In fact, she thought the emotion was really an unfounded excuse for individuals to behave irrationally. However, when she returned to Fellowship Hall after kissing Mrs. Jones goodbye and offering her wishes for an excellent retreat, she found herself reining in the green-eyed monster. What in the world? She thought when she returned and found Jeremiah surrounded by women oooing and ahhing over him, offering their assistance—and obviously more. She could not have left Jeremiah for more than ten minutes. She didn't know if Jeremiah on crutches would've attracted any less attention, but the wheelchair seemed to advertise that he needed to be looked after. Bianca found herself wanting to deck someone—whether that was Jeremiah or one of the women, she wasn't sure. She did know that even when she'd accidentally run into David at a restaurant with his other fiancée--no, one of his other fiancées--her emotions had not been as conflicted as they were now.

Bianca suspected that Jeremiah had sensed her mood when she'd politely asked to be excused as she entered the huddle of women surrounding him because as soon as the women parted to let her through, Jeremiah reached out for her hand and pulled her to his side while simultaneously introducing her to everyone and announcing that while he appreciated their offers, Bianca was taking great care of him. Bianca was both surprised and pleased when Jeremiah asked the women to introduce themselves to her because he didn't remember everyone's name and didn't want to offend anyone. She'd assumed that since the women were being so friendly to Jeremiah, they must be his regular church buddies—or more. But when Jeremiah didn't know their names, she realized that they couldn't be that important to him. One woman--Bianca thought her name was Denise-- appeared to be happy about meeting Bianca. The others were obviously disappointed.

As soon as they were situated in the car a few minutes later, Jeremiah thanked Bianca for rescuing him, which made Bianca laugh out loud.

"It did not look like you needed rescuing, Mr. Jeremiah Alfonso Davis," she responded determined to make light of the situation. She didn't want Jeremiah to know that he had the ability to hurt her so.

"I don't think I like when you say my whole name, Ms. Bianca Denise Jefferson. But I do know that it has been far too long since you kissed me." He then leaned toward Bianca while simultaneously placing his hand on the back of her head and bringing her face toward his.

*****

After they left the church, Bianca stopped at a couple of stores to pick up a few items she knew they needed. Each time they'd stopped, she'd tried to get Jeremiah to remain in the car, but he'd refused. Bianca thought he seemed a little too eager to have her push him around the stores in the wheelchair. She suspected he was up to something, but she couldn't figure out what.

Later that evening while they watched a movie Bianca had selected, Jeremiah wrestled mentally for a way to bring up the situation that had occurred at church. After playing various scenarios in his mind, he decided that the best approach might be to just address the situation directly.

"So are we going to talk about what happened at church today," he asked in a seemingly nonchalant way as he sat with his arm around Bianca's shoulder, "or are we going to act like nothing out of the ordinary happened?"

"What do you mean?" She asked purposely acting as if she couldn't possibly understand what Jeremiah meant.

"I mean, you were kind of upset when you came back to get me after telling Mrs. Jones goodbye. What was that about?"

"I'm not sure what you mean by 'What was that about?'" Bianca countered, continuing the ruse. She had hoped that Jeremiah hadn't noticed the extent to which she'd been upset by the situation, but obviously she'd misjudged his ability to read her moods.

"Look, I don't know what kind of men you've been dealing with, but I love you." Jeremiah placed his hand on Bianca's chin and turned her face towards his. "That means you have my heart and all my attention. Do you understand what that means?"

"I think so." Bianca replied. "I guess I'm just overly sensitive." She mumbled fighting to hold back the tears that fought for release.

"Bianca, I know you were engaged to a jerk who broke your

heart. But I'm not that person. I'm not going to tell you that I won't look at other women. Heck, I'm a man. But we have to have trust if our relationship is going to work." Jeremiah hugged Bianca allowing her head to rest on his shoulder.

After a moment of allowing herself to relish the feeling of just being in Jeremiah's arms, Bianca responded, "I know, Jeremiah…I'm sorry…I just need time to get used to the idea of being with you again." After another moment, she moved from Jeremiah's arms and sat back. Purposely lightening the mood, she added, "And for the record, David cheated on me, but he didn't break my heart. He never had my heart because you still had it."

Jeremiah was both surprised and pleased at Bianca's words. After a brief pause, he asked, "Do you want to talk about it?" He was determined to show Bianca the romance she deserved, but he couldn't seem to bear not touching her. Taking Bianca's hand in his, he added, "I know a little from what Steve told me, but I'd like to hear it from you if you feel like talking about what happened."

Bianca understood why Jeremiah would want to hear the details of her broken engagement from her because she felt the same way about his situation. She knew that Jeremiah had been engaged because Marissa had informed her of that just as Jeremiah had heard about her broken engagement from Steve. Until she heard directly from Jeremiah that he was not still in love with his ex, she'd always wonder whether that person still claimed his heart. Bianca suspected that the same was true for Jeremiah. So she shared the details about how she'd met David, started seeing him, and had eventually accepted his proposal for marriage.

As she told the story to Jeremiah, Bianca recognized for the first time that even though she'd loved David, she'd not been "in love" with David as she was with Jeremiah. She'd been comfortable with David because he hadn't been a threat to her emotions. She hadn't known it then, but she'd realized since seeing Jeremiah again, that no one could've had her heart because Jeremiah still had it. She'd ended their relationship, but she'd never stopped loving him. She acknowledged now that her love for Jeremiah was the reason she'd not been totally devastated when she'd learned of David's affair—no, affairs. She'd learned after her breakup with David that he'd been engaged to at least one other woman besides Bianca and the one she'd met at the restaurant.

"So, I take it you are over this guy, and I have no reason to find him and punish him severely on your behalf?" Jeremiah asked as he kissed the back of her hand which he still clasped when Bianca finished revealing the details of her broken engagement.

"I am definitely over him, and you have no reason to punish him on my behalf." Bianca assured him kissing the back of his hand. "What about you?" She asked after a brief pause. "What happened with you and your ex?"

"Not much." Jeremiah readily offered. "Well, Samantha is her name," he began and then after a short pause, continued. "I guess you can just say we were looking for opposite things. We dated for about a year before I asked her to move in with me. A few months later, I asked her to marry me. I thought I loved her. But now I think I just loved the idea of being loved by someone. I don't want you to get bigheaded or anything, but after you disappeared, I wouldn't let myself get close to any one person. I threw myself into school and then the business. When Samantha and I started seeing one another, I just thought it was time to get on with the rest of my life and settle down."

"I definitely know what you mean about that," Bianca shared. "I felt the same way with David. So what happened?"

"Well, after we got engaged, Samantha would never set a date for the wedding. At first, she just kept saying she couldn't make up her mind. Then one day, she told me she was waiting for me to be promoted so she could marry a vice-president or CEO. When I told her that it wasn't my goal to become either of those, that I was happy being an Operations Manager, everything started to fall apart. We argued almost daily, and she began to find fault with everything I did. Finally, one day, she admitted she'd hooked up with me because she thought I would be a vice-president or CEO. Then she gave me an ultimatum. Either I become a vice-president or CEO at my family's company, or I could work for her dad's company in one of those positions."

"She gave you an ultimatum?" Bianca laughed. "She must not know you very well. I'd think you'd view an ultimatum like I view dares."

"Yeah, well, that's when I decided to leave Dallas and move here. I told my parents I was tired of working inside and wanted to drive again. They thought I was crazy, but I like the freedom of driving. Once we get everything straight with the new office here, I told them I'd take over as long as I can drive periodically."

"Okay. That makes sense. I was wondering how you'd gone from international business wonder boy to long distance truck driver."

"Well, our parents made us learn every arm of the trucking business for two reasons. One, so we would know what each entailed, and two, so we'd know which suited us the most. I can see plusses and minuses in each aspect of the business. I like the freedom to mix things up a bit."

"So how'd Samantha take your leaving?"

"Well, let's just say, she learned pretty quickly what she could do with her ultimatum. I gave her two months to move out of the condo, and then I changed the locks and told the doorman she was not allowed inside again. But that's enough talk about our exes. What's for dessert?" He asked kissing Bianca on the cheek as he released her hand.

"Dessert?" Bianca snickered caught off guard by his request. "Jeremiah, your mind is never far away from your stomach. You can have ice cream, peach cobbler, chocolate cake, or a combination of any of those. I'm having water. I'm watching my weight."

"Your weight is just fine," he called as she headed toward the kitchen. "I'm watching it, too. I'll have peach cobbler and ice cream, thank you."

Bianca smiled to herself as she thought about how quickly and smoothly Jeremiah had changed the mood. She was glad they had talked openly about their exes. Bringing everything out cleared the way for the two of them. Even though Jeremiah and Samantha had only been broken up for a few months, he was adamant that they were finished. That confirmation was just what Bianca needed to hear.

When she brought Jeremiah the warm peach cobbler and vanilla ice cream he'd requested, he'd rewound the movie to the part just before they'd started talking about their exes. They watched the remainder of the movie in a comfortable silence, each one touching the other periodically just because.

*****

As Bianca saw things, the remainder of the week passed as

quickly as possible considering that every day she felt like she was going to explode from the sexual tension that continued to build even though both she and Jeremiah obviously tried to ignore it. The tension was like an elephant in the room that neither of them wanted to discuss. At the beginning of the week, Bianca had revised her writing and exercise schedules and throughout the week she'd followed them precisely to avoid focusing on her growing feelings for Jeremiah as well as to free herself for their date night on Saturday. Actually, it wasn't so much that her feelings for Jeremiah were growing. It was more that the barricade she'd built around her heart ten years ago began to crumble with each hour that she spent in Jeremiah's presence.

Bianca prepared and ate meals with Jeremiah, but between breakfast and dinner she worked on her manuscript. After dinner, the two of them carried on like old friends limiting their physical contact to light touches, holding hands periodically, and engaging in varying levels of heated kisses. Bianca had never thought about the possibility of a human being spontaneously combusting, but she knew that if Jeremiah asked her to help him in the shower again, she'd just strip, jump in the shower, and have her way with him.

While Bianca worked on her manuscript, exercised, and cooked their meals, Jeremiah planned their date for Saturday with the finesse and attention to detail he'd exhibited as operations manager at work. There was no doubt in Jeremiah's mind that his doctor would release him from his medical care during his visit on Friday, so he viewed Saturday as the official beginning of his renewed relationship with Bianca. He was determined that Bianca would experience romance and know that he loved her with all of his heart. She hadn't said it, but he suspected that she might not believe that he was completely over Samantha since they'd only been apart for a few months to her year away from the jerk.

Without Bianca's knowledge, during the week, Jeremiah also exercised his knee without putting weight on it. He wanted to be off crutches and out of the wheelchair as soon as possible after his doctor's visit on Friday, and he was determined to avoid physical therapy visits. He didn't remember all of the exercises he'd done during his recovery period in college after he'd torn his ACL, but he remembered a few basic ones which he did frequently throughout the day. The swelling of his knee had completely subsided, and the pain had diminished, so he felt good about his progress. He iced his knee after each set of exercises, and he was taking only over-the-counter pain meds, which he took in less frequent intervals than when he'd first fallen.

*****

Thursday evening when Mrs. Jones returned from her retreat, she came to visit as she'd promised Bianca. She'd made arrangements with another church member to drop her off at home, so Bianca would not have to pick her up from the church. When Mrs. Jones arrived on Thursday evening, she brought dinner from a restaurant that served home-style healthy meals. While they ate, Mrs. Jones shared highlights from her retreat, and they caught her up on their week's events. Bianca could tell that Mrs. Jones still blamed herself for Jeremiah's fall. She even offered to accompany Jeremiah and Bianca to the visit with the orthopedic specialist the next day, but they both informed her that it was not necessary for her to go. The only way they could convince her not to accompany them was to promise to call her when they left the doctor's office.

*****

The doctor's visit the next day went relatively smoothly. Dr. Phillips was pleased with the way Jeremiah's knee had healed. He even applauded Jeremiah for exercising his knee on his own during the week. Bianca had initially been upset when she'd learned that Jeremiah had been exercising his knee without her knowledge, but she quickly suppressed those feeling because Dr. Phillips obviously approved. He officially released Jeremiah, but he referred him to the physical therapy office located next door for an evaluation and a list of additional exercises which he could do at home over the next few weeks. He also instructed Jeremiah to continue to wear his walking brace for stability over the next two weeks, and he encouraged Jeremiah not to return to work for another two weeks. Bianca was disappointed when Dr. Phillips told Jeremiah to use his own judgment on the issue of when to turn to work. She'd have preferred that the doctor not officially release Jeremiah to return to work until the end of two additional weeks for she expected that Jeremiah would go back to work sooner rather than later. After learning that Jeremiah would be in the physical therapy office for an hour, Bianca informed him that she was going to run to the grocery store to pick up a few items so they'd not have to stop on their way home that afternoon.

While the doctor's visit had gone smoothly, Jeremiah could not say the same thing for the physical therapy visit. The therapist twisted and turned Jeremiah's knee every which way but loose. He informed Jeremiah that he was trying to make sure Jeremiah had full range of motion of his knee. Jeremiah was glad that he'd done some exercising during the past week, for he could only imagine how much additional pain he'd be in if he'd not done at least something to increase the strength and flexibility of his knee on his own. After stretching the muscles, the therapist assigned specific exercises for Jeremiah to do and gave him a printout of exercises he should continue at home over the next three weeks. After Jeremiah completed all of the exercises, the therapist gave him an ice pack to place on his knee for five to ten minutes.

When Bianca returned to the waiting room after her brief shopping trip, Jeremiah was still in the treatment room, so she kept herself busy reading one of the magazines on the table near her chair. When Jeremiah entered the waiting room, he looked whipped. He was drenched in sweat and looked as if he'd just run a marathon. His facial features were contorted into what was obviously a grimace of pain. Bianca was quickly reminded that she was the cause of Jeremiah being hurt, and she winced inwardly. Rising quickly, she went to Jeremiah's side in case he needed her to help him walk. "Jeremiah, are you okay? Do you need to sit down for a minute before we leave?" In that moment she wished she'd made Jeremiah bring the wheelchair.

"No, I'm fine. I just need to get home so I can rest."

~~~~~

CHAPTER THIRTEEN

Exasperated, Bianca took off the third outfit she'd tried on Saturday evening and threw it on top of the pile of clothes on the sofa. If she didn't make a decision quickly, Jeremiah would be back to pick her up, and she'd still be in her underwear. Considering the way Jeremiah had looked when he'd left the physical therapy treatment room the day before, Bianca had expected him to postpone their date night, but he'd insisted that was not an option. He'd told Bianca that he'd been waiting for their official "first date" for almost two weeks and nothing was going to keep them from going. He'd rested and iced his knee Friday afternoon following their return home. Then later that night, he'd completed all of the exercises on the papers the therapist had given him and iced his knee again. As soon as he'd finished breakfast Saturday morning, he'd repeated the routine.

Bianca worried that he might be overworking his knee, but she kept her opinion to herself because she knew Jeremiah hated being coddled. The two of them had spent the morning in each other's company, but Jeremiah had left the house late that afternoon informing Bianca that he'd be back to pick her up for their date at 7:00 PM. He was using one crutch and seemed to be managing well with the stabilizing knee brace that protected his knee but allowed full range of motion.

As she pulled yet another outfit from the closet, Bianca contemplated the fact that she could not understand why she was so nervous. Yes, she was going on a date with Jeremiah, but it wasn't as if this were their real first date. But she had to admit, this date was significant because it was their first date since she'd run away from Jeremiah ten years ago. Even now, she was sure that she'd done the right thing back then, but a part of her had always wondered. Even though she'd been only nineteen at the time, she was certain that she'd been in love with Jeremiah, but how could she have been sure that he was ready to settle down at twenty-one? It was common knowledge that females matured more quickly than males.

After rejecting two more ensembles, Bianca decided on a long sleeved black dress with a v-neckline and a hemline that fell just beneath her knees. Made of a soft stretchy material, the dress accentuated her curves drawing attention to her small waistline. She hadn't planned on going on any dates when she'd packed for her sabbatical, but like most women, she'd brought far more clothes than she needed. To her way of thinking, if she had to pay to check a bag, she'd better get her money's worth.

While Bianca agonized over what to wear, not far outside the Houston city limits, Jeremiah completed the last details of the romantic evening he'd planned just for her. He was determined to give Bianca all of the romance she deserved, and tonight marked the first of a lifetime of events. He chuckled to himself as he thought of the saying his mom always repeated to him and his brothers. He couldn't remember the exact words, but basically the saying meant that the same thing it took to get a wife was the same thing it took to keep her. Jeremiah had lost Bianca once. He had no intention of losing her again. He preferred to think of that saying about loving something and letting it go and it coming back to you forever.

When Jeremiah returned to the house to pick Bianca up, the door to the den was closed, so he assumed Bianca was still getting ready. The sweet flowery smell in the house led him to believe that she'd recently left the guest bathroom. When Bianca opened the door to the den and walked into the family room, Jeremiah glanced over his shoulder while simultaneously turning off the television with the remote. He was so shocked when he saw her that he dropped the remote onto the floor. Quickly picking it up while he regained his composure, he used all of his energy not to gape at Bianca.

Jeremiah had no doubts that Bianca was oblivious to how sexy she looked in what was probably a simple black dress on a hanger but became far more than that on Bianca's shapely body. The pearl necklace, earrings and bracelet added a sense of demureness to the dress, but just barely. Bianca wore her hair in some sort of up-do with tendrils hanging on one side and her bangs swooped behind her ear on the other side. The simple black pumps accentuated the toned calf muscles of her bare legs. Throughout the past two weeks, Jeremiah hadn't seen Bianca in a dress. Her daily attire included jeans, sweat pants, or workout wear. Even on Sunday, she'd worn slacks and a blouse to church. It occurred to Jeremiah that he'd not seen Bianca in a dress in over ten years. In the clingy black dress, it was even more evident that Bianca had become more shapely, more womanly, in their time apart. He hoped the heels on Bianca's pumps would not cause her any problems tonight because he really liked what they did for her legs.

Jeremiah suspected that Bianca was unaware of the effect she had on the opposite sex. On the sexiness meter, she measured twenty on a scale of one to ten without even trying. While many women spent hours in front of a mirror trying to achieve a certain look, Bianca woke with that look. Once he was sure he could be close to Bianca without embarrassing himself, Jeremiah crossed the room to Bianca and kissed her lightly on the lips. He knew that if he kissed her the way he wanted to, they'd not make it out of the house.

"You look beautiful! Where've you been hiding that dress?" He asked taking her hand and twirling her.

"It's just been hanging in the closet. I haven't been anywhere to wear it before tonight. You look mighty handsome yourself. I don't think I've seen you in a suit since your graduation party where we met," she added laughing.

"Too bad my knee won't let me dance tonight. I'll just have to make up an excuse to hold you close. Let's go before we don't go," he kissed her on the cheek and offered Bianca the crook of his arm.

When they exited the house, Bianca was surprised to see a late model Mercedes luxury sedan in the driveway where Jeremiah normally parked his truck.

"Where did you get this car?" She asked as Jeremiah opened the passenger front door for her.

"This, my dear, is one of my other cars."

"One of your other cars," Bianca teased when Jeremiah had opened the driver's side door and seated himself.

"Yes. You know my affinity for cars. I also have a 1967 Mustang I'm restoring."

"Well, I'll say..." She hadn't thought about Jeremiah's love of cars or the Mustang he'd driven the summer they'd met in a while. "So where are we going for dinner?"

"That, my dear, is a surprise."

*****

Bianca was so tense during the drive to the restaurant that she could not have duplicated the route on her own to save her life. Throughout the trip she couldn't get out of her mind the look on Jeremiah's face when she'd entered the family room. First, his eyes had opened widely indicating surprise or shock. Then they'd narrowed to slits, but not before she'd observed his desire for her. Even after everything they'd gone through the past couple of weeks, Bianca still found it difficult to believe the effect she had on Jeremiah.

When Jeremiah exited the highway, it occurred to Bianca that they seemed to have left all restaurants behind with the street lights, but after a few minutes of driving in pitch blackness, Bianca saw what must be the restaurant lights in the distance.

"How in the heck did you find this place, way out here?" She asked turning toward Jeremiah.

"I have it on good authority, that this place is great," Jeremiah responded.

As Jeremiah closed the distance to the building, Bianca realized the structure was not a restaurant at all. They were at Jeremiah's new home. It had been the middle of the day when they'd visited with Jeremiah's family the previous week; everything looked entirely different at night.

"Oh, Jeremiah, it looks beautiful all lit up."

"You said you wanted to see it first with me, so here we are." Jeremiah stated as he put the car in park and turned off the engine in the driveway. He hadn't realized until that moment how much it mattered to him what Bianca thought of his home. The home he'd already begun to think of as their home.

Jeremiah exited the Mercedes and walked around to Bianca's side to open her door. Once Bianca was out of the car, Jeremiah closed her door and held out his bent arm for Bianca to grasp. "If you need me to carry you in because of those heels, let me know," Jeremiah offered.

"I should be fine. The ground is not too bumpy. And I wouldn't let you carry me with your bad knee, anyway."

The ground was bare and somewhat rocky, but even city girl,

Bianca, could imagine the yard beautifully landscaped.

Flood lights highlighted the home making it appear as an enormous structure amidst the nearly pitch darkness surrounding it. Bianca remembered that Jeremiah's new home was one level, but she'd purposely not paid much attention to it when they'd come with his family the previous week. As she'd told Jeremiah that day, she wanted to see his home for the first time with him.

When Jeremiah opened the front door, Bianca thought she was going crazy when she heard smooth jazz music playing, but as soon as she entered the vast foyer, she identified the source which immediately brought tears to her eyes.

"That is not the effect I was going for," Jeremiah leaned down and whispered to in her ear.

"Oh, Jeremiah, It's so perfect. Give me a minute... I was so not expecting this."

"Here, take this," Jeremiah said as he handed Bianca the handkerchief from his jacket pocket.

A jazz trio consisting of a woman playing a saxophone, a man on a keyboard, and a second man playing an upright bass stood on the other side of what had to be the largest family room Bianca had ever seen. Bianca suspected that the hardwood floor in the almost empty room contributed to its massive appearance. Between the musicians and where she and Jeremiah stood, a single table set for two highlighted by candles burning added to the ambiance. The wall behind the musicians appeared to be made of glass. On closer inspection, Bianca, saw that the wall was really a bank of windows that actually covered three walls which made Bianca think that the family room led directly into a sunroom. The musicians' instruments blocked the doorway, so she couldn't tell for sure.

"Do you want dinner or your tour first?" Jeremiah asked, interrupting Bianca's thoughts.

"The tour, for sure."

"For that, we need lights," he stated before flipping switches on the wall nearest him.

When Jeremiah had turned on the lights, Bianca took in the open design of the family room and immediately recognized some of the elements she and Jeremiah had discussed years ago as part of a dream home. To the left of the family room sat an open kitchen fit for a chef, complete with granite counter tops, a cooking peninsula, and circular breakfast bar in the center of the room. On the far right side of the family room, a fire burned in a fireplace built of stone.

"Oh, Jeremiah, it's beautiful!" She exclaimed in awe. "You remembered."

"I hadn't realized it. But I guess I did. We'll start in the master suite and work our way back."

Throughout the tour, the musicians continued to play. After Bianca and Jeremiah toured the master suite which consisted of a sitting room, master bedroom, matching his and her bathrooms, both containing walk in closets, Jeremiah led Bianca to a room obviously designed to serve as a library or office. With floor-to-ceiling bookshelves on all four walls and a desk protruding from one of the bookcases, Bianca thought it was a great place to curl up with a book or to grade papers. She could already envision a chaise lounge placed in the center of the room.

When they left the library, Jeremiah directed Bianca to the powder room which was to the left of the front door and then to the kitchen. To the left of the kitchen on the front of the house twin bedrooms were separated by a full bath accessible from both bedrooms making their location perfect for children. To the left of the kitchen on the back of the house, a full size laundry room led to a four-car garage. On the other side of the garage was a three room guest suite consisting of a bedroom with a fire place, walk-in closet, sitting room, and full bath.

When Jeremiah brought Bianca back to the kitchen, she saw that a chef and waiter in full uniforms awaited them. She wondered where they'd been hiding and was once again overcome with emotions. No one had ever gone to such lengths to please her before.

"Sir, whenever you and the lady are ready, dinner will be served," the waiter said to Jeremiah.

"Thank you, Pierre. Bianca, allow me to introduce Pierre Jamison our waiter for this evening and Chef Roman Allen."

"I am pleased to meet both of you," Bianca stated after both men had greeted her and shaken her hand. "This is so special. I feel honored." Turning to Jeremiah, she continued as the men resumed their duties. "Jeremiah, thank you. I can't believe you did all of this for me."

"I told you. You deserve the best. We can wash up in the

powder room, you first. And then we'll have dinner. Chef Allen prepared one of his specialties, almond crusted salmon with caramelized onions and some other things I can't remember."

Gazing at her reflection in the mirror in the powder room, Bianca acknowledged that she was truly overwhelmed with everything. Jeremiah's home was so beautiful, and the fact that he'd included components they'd discussed over ten years ago touched a special place in her heart. And the time Jeremiah had put into planning this date for her spoke volumes. She'd never had anyone to hire musicians, a chef, and a waiter for her. Jeremiah had gone to great lengths to make her feel extra special. Dabbing at her eyes again, she quickly washed her hands and returned to the foyer where she waited for Jeremiah while he washed his hands.

When Jeremiah returned to her side, he took Bianca's hand and led her to the table situated in the middle of the room. Bianca noted that even though Jeremiah had used his crutch throughout the tour, he'd left it by the front door before entering the powder room. When they reached the table, Jeremiah pulled Bianca's chair out and seated her before moving to the other side of the table to sit directly across from her.

As soon as they were seated, Bianca noticed that the candles on the table were actually flameless, but that didn't take away from the mood. Pierre approached their table with the wine selection and asked which they preferred. The choices were a brut champagne and a red moscato wine. Jeremiah let Bianca choose not surprised when she selected the latter which his sisters also preferred. Pierre poured Jeremiah's wine first allowing him to test it before giving his approval. Then Pierre poured wine for both of them.

"To us," Jeremiah said raising his glass in the air as soon as Pierre left the table.

"To us," Bianca responded.

Throughout dinner which consisted of mixed greens salads followed by their entrees of the salmon dish, Jeremiah and Bianca chatted. To Bianca, it was if they'd been transported to the past when they'd loved one another freely and talked about everything. Chef Allen came to their table to ask about the meal midway through the entree. Jeremiah and Bianca both assured him everything was superb. During their meal, Bianca asked Jeremiah how he'd been able to arrange their romantic date in his home before actually closing on the house. Jeremiah explained that the county building inspector had given him the okay to move in just that week, so he assured her she didn't have to worry about their being arrested. He also shared with her how he'd come to buy the land and build the house with his own money, mostly from the college fund his parents had started for him. He informed Bianca that because of his scholarships for undergraduate and graduate school, he hadn't spent much of the money his parents had saved for his education. Instead, he'd invested the bulk of that money and had added to it over the years amassing a decent amount of money to purchase the land, build, and furnish his home. Bianca was both surprised and honored when he asked her if she'd be willing to help him shop for furniture that next week.

While Jeremiah and Bianca enjoyed their dessert of chocolate mousse with strawberries and whipped cream served with decaf coffee, the musicians took a break and came to the table to introduce themselves to Bianca. Bianca thanked each of them and complimented them on their talent. Sonya asked Bianca if there were anything in particular she wanted to hear, but Bianca assured her they were doing just fine with their selections. The trio played a few more songs after reassembling, and shortly afterward everyone left the house, leaving Jeremiah and Bianca alone. It took Bianca a few minutes after everyone had left to realize that music continued to play. In response to her inquisitive look, Jeremiah told her about the built in stereo system. He also shared that the musicians had left one of their own compact discs playing for their enjoyment.

Jeremiah was caught totally off guard when Bianca stood up, walked to his side of the table and kissed him smack dab on the lips before returning to her seat. He was speechless. This was the first time Bianca had actually initiated kissing him. She always responded to his advances, but she'd never made the first move.

"Thank you for planning this beautiful evening for me, Jeremiah. I can't tell you how special you've made me feel."

"You are special, Bianca. And anything I can do to help you know that I will do. And by the way, feel free to kiss me anytime you feel like. Finish your dessert. I want to show you my favorite spot in the house." Jeremiah announced.

"We can go now. I can't eat another bite," Bianca responded as she wiped her mouth with her napkin and placed it on the table.

Rising from the table, and taking Bianca's hand, Jeremiah led her to the other side of the family room to a huge chocolate brown reclining chaise lounge situated in the center of the room behind where the musicians had been playing. Bianca hadn't even seen the chair behind the musicians and their instruments. In fact, the musicians and their instruments had hidden most of what had been behind them from her view.

Now, Bianca could see that the family room did lead into a sunroom as she'd initially thought. The sunroom was connected to the main structure of the house on one wall and extended at least thirty feet out with floor-to-ceiling windows on three of the walls. After indicating to Bianca to have a seat in the chaise lounge, Jeremiah walked to the other side, sat down beside her, and wrapped his arms around her shoulders before using the lever to recline the chair.

"This is your favorite spot in the house, Jeremiah?" Bianca asked clearly puzzled when they were lying flat on their backs.

"Wait for it," Jeremiah responded kissing Bianca on the cheek before taking a remote from the pocket on his side of the chair and pushing buttons.

Right before her eyes, the ceiling of the room slid back revealing open panes of glass. She had been mistaken. This room wasn't a sunroom, it was a solarium. With the ceiling shade retracted, the moon and stars lit up the room. "Awesome! Wow! It's like we're outside. I think I can actually identify constellations we studied in school. I see why it's your favorite spot in the house," she declared snuggling into Jeremiah. "You bought this chair just for this purpose."

"I did indeed," he said turning toward Bianca and resting on one arm. "I don't know if you have any idea how much I love you. But, Bianca, I want you to know this night is only the beginning for us. You deserve only the best, and I intend to give it to you every day of your life."

For the second time that night, Bianca initiated a kiss. Only this time, it wasn't a quick peck on Jeremiah's lips.

~~~~~

CHAPTER FOURTEEN

As Bianca looked around the banquet hall Friday night, she was pleased with how everything had come together for Marissa and Steve's annual pre-Thanksgiving party. Her friends had returned from Paris Monday afternoon, and Marissa and Bianca had literally hit the ground running on the last minute details for the party. When Mrs. Jones had informed Bianca that Marissa had been planning the party for months before she left, Mrs. Jones had predicted the party would go on without a hitch even if Marissa and Steve missed it.

However, in spite of all the work Marissa had put into planning the party before she'd left the country, Bianca still found that helping Marissa with the last minute details of her party had been more difficult than helping Jeremiah furnish his entire home in a week. Of course, shopping for furniture with an almost unlimited budget had added to her ecstasy. And Bianca did have to admit, even if only to herself, that she loved shopping more than event planning which was Marissa's forte. Bianca's favorite part of the hectic week had been shopping for her dress and shoes for tonight.

Bianca's least favorite part of the week had been spending the last three days away from Jeremiah. With her impending departure back to Chicago, she would've preferred that Jeremiah wait until she'd left before he returned to work. She also wished he'd waited the full two weeks recommended by Dr. Phillips. But at least now she'd know firsthand how he handled driving long distances. Jeremiah had purposely planned a short trip from Wednesday to Friday to ease back into work, but as Bianca saw it, the three extra days would've provided them with at least a few additional stolen moments. Plus, she'd be leaving on Monday, and they still hadn't discussed where they were headed or when they'd see each other again.

The party had only gotten started about an hour ago, but the banquet hall was already filling up. As Bianca scanned the room, it seemed to her that everyone was having a great time. The caterers had done a great job on the food, and the disc jockey played a variety of music which kept the dance floor full. Bianca couldn't see Marissa or Steve from where she stood. She suspected Marissa was off tending to some minute detail. If Steve wasn't visiting with one of their guests, he was on a mission for Marissa.

Her friends had met and fallen in love while they were in high school and Bianca had witnessed their love grow stronger over the years. Bianca prayed that she and Jeremiah could have a relationship even half as solid as Marissa and Steve's. She wanted to trust what she felt in her heart, but all her life she'd relied on her brain. Even though her mom always told Bianca and her sisters to follow their hearts, Bianca had spent her whole life thinking her way out of everything, generally discounting her emotions for what they were— pure feelings—and therefore not to be trusted. She was determined to let her heart take the lead regarding all matters related to Jeremiah. She loved him, and she believed he loved her. But was their love strong enough to withstand the test of time? The fact that it had survived the ten years they'd been apart was a positive sign to Bianca. Right now she just needed Jeremiah to arrive at the party.

Once again, Bianca checked the time on her iPhone while simultaneously looking for another text message from Jeremiah. He'd sent the last one from a rest stop two hours ago that said he was about three hours away. Finding no new messages, she quickly entered the ladies room to use the facilities and refresh her makeup in anticipation of his arrival. She and Jeremiah had agreed that Jeremiah would drive straight to the house, shower and dress, and come directly to the banquet hall. For him, Marissa and Steve's Annual Pre-Thanksgiving Party was a regularly attended event. For Bianca, it was a first. Once again, Bianca thanked fate for allowing her to participate this year when she'd never been able to attend in the past. Till now, she'd only experienced the event vicariously through pictures and stories from Marissa and Steve as well as from their family and friends over the years. This year she'd experience the event personally.

When Bianca entered the restroom, all of the stalls were occupied, but a moment later a women exited one. Bianca greeted the woman and slipped into the stall as the other woman activated the faucet on the sink. Bianca had just locked the door when she heard another stall open.

"Hey, Girl! What are you doing here?"

"Hey, Krissy. How are you, girl? You know I come to Jeremiah's cousin's party every year."

"I thought you and Jeremiah broke up?"

"Where'd you hear that? We've just been taking a break."

Under normal circumstances, Bianca would not have paid any attention to the chatter in the women's room. But when she heard Jeremiah's name, she was instantly on the alert. How many people could Steve know named Jeremiah who had recently broken up with someone?

"Really? That is not what I was told."

"Girl, you know you can't believe everything you hear. Come on. Let's check out the buffet table. They always have the best food."

Bianca was stunned. She could not believe what she'd just heard. Clearly, the women who was not Krissy, had to be Samantha. Jeremiah's Samantha. But Jeremiah had insisted that he and Samantha had broken up for good. What kind of miscommunication could've occurred for Samantha to think she and Jeremiah were just taking a break? When Bianca exited the ladies room, she immediately went to find Marissa. On the way, she passed the woman she'd greeted in the restroom. That woman was talking with another woman now. Bianca didn't know if the woman she'd greeted was Jeremiah's Samantha or Krissy. She also didn't know if the woman she'd greeted was talking to the same other woman from the restroom or to someone else. All she knew was that Samantha was here at the party.

Scanning the room quickly Bianca located Marissa talking to Steve on the other side of the banquet hall. Even from where she stood, Bianca could tell that Marissa and Steve were engaged in a heated argument although they'd not raised their voices. When Steve saw Bianca looking in their direction, he motioned for her to join them. As soon as Bianca reached them, Steve kissed Marissa on the cheek and walked away after first telling Bianca to talk to her friend.

"Are you okay? What's the matter?" Bianca asked.

"I cannot believe that woman had the audacity to come to our party!" Marissa exclaimed in a whisper as she nodded in the direction of a group of four women seated at one of the bistro tables in the room.

"I know…Samantha. I just heard while I was in the ladies' room." Bianca looked in the direction Marissa indicated. The women from the bathroom was now seated at a bistro table with the same women she'd been talking to when Bianca had exited the bathroom and two other women. Bianca quickly surmised that the unknown woman from the bathroom had to be Samantha because now she flagrantly waved her left hand in the air as she engaged in what appeared to be an overly animated conversation with the other women.

"I told Steve he needed to go over there and tell her to leave, or I would."

"Girl, you don't have to tell her to leave." Bianca stated with more bravado than she felt. "Everything will be fine. The last thing you want to do is cause a scene."

"Now you know I don't mind causing a scene." Marissa gave Bianca a look that would melt butter. "That woman just showed up here to cause trouble for Jeremiah, and I'm not going to let her do that to him or to you. You two deserve the chance to work things out after all these years."

"Marissa, just calm down, and let it go." Bianca hugged Marissa trying to calm her. "Don't worry about me. Your making a big deal about it will only make things worse. Let's just enjoy your party. Remember, this is my first time at one of your infamous parties." Bianca hoped that the laugh she added sounded more real than it felt. The last thing she wanted to do was to let Marissa know how truly upset she was. Bianca had witnessed Marissa's protectiveness of her friends on more than one occasion while they'd been in college. She didn't want to do anything to encourage Marissa to go there tonight.

"Oh, Bianca, I'm sorry. I forgot. It's just that you and Jeremiah need time to work on your relationship without all of this added drama."

"I know. We'll work it out as soon as Jeremiah gets here." Offering her arm to Marissa, Bianca calmly asked, "Why don't you take me around and introduce me to everyone I don't know?" Bianca knew that Marissa took entertaining personally, and she hoped that encouraging Marissa to return to her role as hostess would keep her from focusing on the fact that Jeremiah's ex had crashed her party. As the two of them walked around the room chatting with guests, Bianca could feel the tension in Marissa's body dissipate. At one point, Steve walked up and hugged both of them before whispering "thank you" in Bianca's ear.

Bianca wanted to believe that everything would work out as she'd told Marissa. But for real, she didn't know what to expect. Jeremiah had told her that he no longer loved Samantha. But what if his absence from Samantha had made his love grow stronger? What if when he saw Samantha, his feelings all came tumbling back into his heart? When Bianca had first overheard the exchange of words in the ladies' room, her first response had been to run. But she'd convinced herself that running wouldn't solve anything. She'd experienced running from Jeremiah once before, only to come full circle. This time she was going to face the situation head on. Jeremiah had said he'd be at the party, so she'd wait. He'd said he loved her and wanted to spend the rest of his life with her. Why should she believe anything she'd heard from this woman she'd just seen for the first time?

The fact that Marissa was pissed Samantha had showed up at the party fueled Bianca's confidence in the situation. Samantha had obviously not been invited to the party. However, for whatever reason, Samantha believed she had a right to be at the party. She also believed she and Jeremiah had been merely taking a vacation from one another. Only Jeremiah could set the record straight. He had to be here any minute. If Bianca discovered that Samantha was right, then, and only then, would she leave and go back to Chicago. Only then.

Each time the door to the banquet hall opened, Bianca looked toward the door. Each time another guest who was not Jeremiah entered, her spirits waned.

*****

Jeremiah hated to admit it, but his mom and Bianca had been right. He should have waited the full two weeks recommended by Dr. Phillips before going back on the road. It wasn't so much that his knee still bothered him too much, but he was exhausted. The surgeon had warned Jeremiah that sitting with his knee in one position for long periods of time, as with driving, would cause the muscles to spasm. Jeremiah had assured the doctor that he'd take frequent rest stops and would gradually increase the time he drove without stretching the muscles. The doctor had not told Jeremiah that his entire body would ache from sitting in the truck for long hours. The additional five days at home would've allowed Jeremiah to build his strength back up with the exercises the physical therapist had given him. And on top of that, the real deal was that he missed Bianca. They were just getting to the point where he felt that she was ready to fully commit to a relationship with him. He felt that she needed a little more time, but he didn't have much time with her returning to Chicago the next week.

Although they'd declared their love for one another, they hadn't really discussed what happened next. Jeremiah was determined that they'd do that tonight. It might be after Steve and Marissa's party, or it might be during the party, but they were going to have a serious talk tonight. Jeremiah couldn't wait to get back to Houston so that he could shower and shave and meet Bianca at the party. If he hadn't taken his current assignment, he'd have been at the house and would've taken Bianca to the party. Instead, because he'd insisted on getting back to work, they had to settle for meeting at the party. At least Bianca would ride home from the party with him.

When Jeremiah arrived at the banquet hall, all he could think about was taking Bianca into his arms and kissing her senseless. As he walked from the parking lot to the entrance, he could hear the music growing louder the closer he got to the door.

*****

When Jeremiah finally arrived, Bianca saw him pan the room immediately upon entering the hall. When their gazes connected, it was if the noise from the party evaporated and everything began to move in slow motion. Simultaneously, the two of them started walking toward one another. Bianca could hear her heartbeat pounding in her ears. Just before she and Jeremiah reached one another, Bianca heard Samantha call Jeremiah's name, and she saw Jeremiah glance in Samantha's direction before looking back at her. The look on Jeremiah's face during that brief interlude told Bianca all she needed to know.

When Jeremiah reached Bianca, he gathered her into his arms and kissed her as if they'd been apart longer than the three days it had been.

"Jeremiah, what are you doing kissing that b…witch? I'm the

one wearing your ring!" Samantha exclaimed hysterically waiving her left hand in the air as she'd been doing when Bianca had first figured out who she was. "You know you love me. We were just taking a break. You're just trying to make me jealous."

Jeremiah couldn't believe that Samantha was carrying on as she was doing. First of all, he couldn't believe that she'd shown up at Steve and Marissa's party uninvited. How long had she been there? And what in the world must Bianca be thinking? He had hoped that when Samantha saw him kissing Bianca, she'd leave the party and his life quietly. But no...Now, she was yelling at him like a crazy woman. Jeremiah could only think of one way to stop Samantha's antics. He'd planned to talk to Bianca before the evening was over, but it looked like now was the best time.

Ending their kiss, Jeremiah removed his arms from around Bianca and took her left hand in his as he kneeled on his good knee.

"Jeremiah, are you okay?" Bianca asked initially thinking his injured knee had given out on him.

"Bianca Denise Jefferson, I have been in love with you for ten years. Will you take me, Jeremiah Alfonso Davis, to be your lawfully wedded husband till death do us part? I promise to honor and obey you and forsake all others." As he spoke, Jeremiah pulled a ring box from his suit jacket pocket, opened the box, removed the ring and placed it on Bianca's left ring finger. "I was going to give this to you ten years ago, but .... Oh yeah, and I already asked your mom and dad, and they said it's okay."

Bianca could barely see for the tears in her eyes. Everything was happening so quickly. As she looked at the solitaire glistening on her finger, she was overwhelmed with love and happiness. Pulling Jeremiah up, she placed her hands on his cheeks and kissed him again.

Interrupting their kiss, he asked, "Is that a yes?"

"That is indeed a 'yes'," she answered. "Definitely, a 'yes'." As Bianca allowed Jeremiah to gather her in his arms again, the party guests cheered. Neither Bianca nor Jeremiah heard the banquet hall door close behind Samantha.

~~~~~

EPILOGUE

The sun peeking through the blinds woke Bianca. Shifting away from its rays, she allowed herself a moment to get her bearings. So much had happened in the last seven months she still found herself reeling. She'd gone home the Monday after Jeremiah's proposal as planned. But Jeremiah had joined her later that week for the family Thanksgiving dinner at her mom's. Celeste and Mark had flown in from Italy, and Serena and Darnell had come from Washington, DC. Even their dad had come. Of course, it had been no surprise to Bianca that everyone had fallen in love with Jeremiah.

She and Jeremiah had decided to get married immediately, but they'd agreed to have a traditional wedding ceremony in the summer. To all outside the family, tomorrow was her and Jeremiah's official wedding day, but her family and his had already witnessed that special event right here in their new home on New Year's Eve. Beneath the stars and the moon shining through the glass ceiling of the solarium, they'd said their vows to one another long before they'd rung in the new year.

Jeremiah had called the solarium his favorite spot in the house the first night he'd brought Bianca inside his new home. Since that time, Bianca had added it to her list of special places, but she really didn't have one that stood out. Jeremiah had simply done a fabulous job planning and overseeing the building of his home, their home now. Bianca still smiled every time she remembered how they'd christened the oversize reclining chaise lounge when Jeremiah had first shown her the receding shade ceiling of the solarium. Periodically, they returned to that same spot. Just last night, or was it early this morning, they'd had a repeat performance. They had literally stumbled to bed just as the sun had made its way onto the horizon.

Bianca could hardly believe that she and Jeremiah had flown back and forth visiting one another for six months before she'd been able to officially move in at the end of May when her school year had ended. Starting in the fall, she'd be teaching online courses for her college back home though she'd have to travel there periodically for required meetings. Her mom had been especially pleased that Bianca's job would require her to travel home fairly regularly. The icing on the cake was that her manuscript had been accepted by her publisher, and she'd been given a release date.

Glancing at the clock, Bianca acknowledged that she'd better get a move on it if she planned to feed Jeremiah breakfast before her sisters swooped her up for the pre-wedding day events they'd put on her agenda. Mentally, Bianca ticked off the list of things she had to do before her sisters arrived. Just as she rolled over to go take her shower, Jeremiah wrapped his arm across her naked body.

"Not yet," he whispered. I'm not ready for you to leave me yet."

"Jeremiah, you act like I'm running away from home. I don't leave for a couple of hours, and then tomorrow you'll have me all to yourself again."

"I just need a little something to tide me over," he insisted capturing her lips with his.

Bianca thought she had a clear argument in her mind, but as soon as Jeremiah's tongue parted her lips, she knew she was a goner. No matter how many times they made love, Jeremiah had the ability to make her melt with just one look. When he touched her or kissed her, she had no will power whatsoever.

Jeremiah brought his hand to her breast and began to fondle her already taut nipple while deepening his kiss. Bianca heard herself groan as she simultaneously brought her arms around Jeremiah and repositioned their bodies so that she lay beneath him. Jeremiah removed his lips from hers and quickly found the nipple he'd been fondling. Soon he began taking turns lathing first one nipple and then the other while concurrently caressing her breasts. Bianca arched against Jeremiah relishing the feel of his taut body against her curves. She felt his hands move down her body kneading her most sensitive spots along the way. Surprisingly, she was already moist. She could feel him close to her entrance. It never ceased to amaze her that she could affect him so. The fact that she did aroused her even more.

Shifting, she began her own ministrations starting with his nipples and working her way down. Bianca thought she'd pass out from waiting for Jeremiah to claim her, but Jeremiah seemed intent on making her writhe in ecstasy. Just when Bianca thought she could take it no more, Jeremiah guided himself inside her.

Together they recreated the rhythm as ancient as time itself. It was as if two melded into one as their heart rates increased in sync with one another. Time stood still. Time sped up. Bianca shifted to allow Jeremiah to penetrate more deeply as she wrapped her feet around his calves. Minute by minute, the intensity increased until simultaneously they reached their pinnacle. Immediately, Jeremiah attempted to adjust his position to remove his weight from Bianca, but she tightened her legs, not yet ready to break their connection.

Sated, they lay still until their breathing returned to normal. Just when Jeremiah thought he'd drift off to sleep, Bianca began making tiny circles up and down his back with both hands. "If you plan on going anywhere," he warned, "I advise you to stop that." When Bianca giggled like a teenager, Jeremiah knew she'd been taunting him on purpose. He shook his head as he acknowledged silently that he could only blame himself for awakening Bianca to her sexual prowess.

###

ABOUT THE AUTHOR

"If you love somebody, let them go, for if they return, they were always yours. If they don't, they never were." Kahlil Gibran

B.K. Jonas is a romantic at heart and because of this, she has always been drawn to second chance love stories. She's an avid reader of romance, has been writing for fun since she was a child and has been teaching writing all of her adult life. A transplanted midwesterner who lives in North Carolina with husband, B. K. Jonas loves to travel and spend time with family and friends. She and her husband are the proud parents of two daughters and honored grandparents of six grandsons and one granddaughter. *Fate's Rendevous* is her debut romance novel.

CONNECT WITH B. K. JONAS

Thank you for reading *Fate's Rendezvous*. If you enjoyed reading Bianca and Jeremiah's story as much as I enjoyed writing it, I trust that you will also enjoy reading my upcoming novels in the A Dallas Davis Romance series.

Connect with me on the following social media:

Friend me on Facebook: http://www.facebook.com/B.K.Jonas

Visit my website: http://www.B.K.Jonas.com

FATE'S Rendezvous
Discussion Guide

1. Who is your favorite *FATE's Rendezvous* character and why?

2. What was your reaction to Bianca letting Mrs. Jones believe that she and Jeremiah had just met? How else could Bianca have handled that situation?

3. We often run away from our fears like Bianca did ten years ago. If you had been friends with Bianca back then, what advice would you have given her?

4. Bianca's mom always told her daughers to follow their hearts. What advice have you received or given regarding matters of the heart?

5. What is Bianca's most endearing personality trait? Why?

6. What is Jeremiah's most endearing personality trait? Why?

7. How would you have reacted to the situation Bianca encountered after lunch with Jeremiah at the church?

8. Marissa was quite upset by Samantha crashing her party, but Bianca helped her to maintain her composure. How would you have reacted in a similar situation? Why?

9. We often have to overcome personal insecurities to accomplish our goals. Describe a time when you had to overcome personal insecurities. How did you accomplish overcoming your personal insecurities?

10. Who would you like to read more about in upcoming novels in the "Loving a Dallas Davis" series?

www.ingramcontent.com/pod-product-compliance
Lightning Source LLC
Chambersburg PA
CBHW020246150626
46552CB00020B/526